HAVEN HOUSE

AN AUTOMATON NOVEL

Imogene Nix

Please note:

The UK and USA share the English language, but there are many words that are spelled differently. Some words have extra letters in the British spelling, such as the word cancelled. In American English, it is spelled canceled. There also words that interchange the letters c or s and sometimes z. For example, in America, you spell offense and in Britain, it is written as offence. We also use the letter u in many words, such as colour and flavour.

These spellings are **not** incorrect.

This book is written in UK English to reflect my Australian/English background.

Cover Art by Dexpress Covers

Editing by Hot Tree Editing

EBook ISBN 978-1-922369-49-9

Paperback ISBN 978-1-922369-50-5

Glossary

Note: As this series is built on a Steampunk reality (historical) some of the terms may be unusual. The ones listed below are those you may see referenced throughout the Automatons series. This list is not exhaustive, but lists the majority of commonly used terms.

Aeroship/Airship—steampunk aircraft, normally associated with commercial or privately owned passenger and freight ships.

Aeronaut—pilot.

Apothecary—a person who prepares and sells medicines and drugs. Not a doctor, but more a chemist.

Artificer—skilled worker; craftsperson; one who contrives, devises, or constructs something.

Chronometer—clock or watch.

Datascope—an analytical engine (computer) with a screen to access the data. May be portable or desk-sized.

Datascreen—device to read data on a datascope or analytical engine, consisting of a flat surface displaying text and/or images generated by tightly focused aether rays lighting up tiny receptors on the back of the screen.

Decoction—an extraction or essence of something, obtained by boiling it down. Usually used when describing medications.

Dirigible— see aeroship/airship.

Hermetic—Completely sealed, especially against the escape or entry of air.

House—a central location, relating to the Cults. Ie Haven House or Nobel Crest

Laudanum—an opiate, freely available in an apothecary. Pain reliever. Addictive.

Marconi—device for communication through the air, a radio receiver.

Ocular—a single eyepiece of an optical instrument. For example a telescope or microscope, unlike binoculars (having two lenses).

Physiotraducere— a doctor/medical professional who specialises in the replacement of limbs requiring the use of cogs to replace musculatory systems.

Prong Wheels— special cogs manufactured from copper and treated for use in the body. Each is marked with a symbol, ensuring we know they were used by a Physiotraducere - and particularly searchable by number.

Tincture—alcohol solution of a nonvolatile medicine, e.g., tincture of iodine.

Water Closet—lavatory. A toilet.

Wireless Transmitter—a device for sending or broadcasting communications through the air. Communications are received by a radio (receiver) device. See *Marconi*.

Wireless Power Transmitter—device designed to deliver electrical current to distant devices through the air; e.g., a Tesla coil.

Wireless Telegraph—sends and receives communication through the air. Transmitter and receiver.

Prologue

Dearest Diary,

For so many years, I've avoided remembering and writing the story of my life. Too many hurts have grown and festered, and I've struggled to find the good that exists to ease my mind. My husband suggested I should set myself goals in life. Things I wish to achieve and good deeds I may carry out to wash away the hurts I carry.

Once free of these painful weights, we might conceive a child of love after all the years of trying without success.

I've settled on the first. It's also the most important to my mind.

I remember the first time I met Amaryllis Coultihan.

She'd been brought into the house. Yet another of the strays "bought" by my brother and father for the purposes of populating Haven Town, a blip on the map near Ericksville, in the state of Scottsvale. She'd been a little girl of maybe six or seven, though small for her size when Master purchased her from a farmer who could no longer care for his brood of children. He'd made the choice to ensure a better life for her—or so he thought—but it had turned out differently, unfortunately.

They weren't local. Not until later on.

I remember that day. Vividly. The way Master had smiled, and the little girl's silent tears. I was old enough to understand what was happening, and it was like a punch to the chest.

There wasn't an ounce of good in the transactions Master and Junior, as my brother was coming to be known, undertook. All I could see was more misery. My father had bought and discarded more women and children than I could count, long before I ran away.

On my return to Haven Town, with the husband of my choice, I realised my brother, Travis Haven III, continued our father's vision of a town set aside from time and the greater community and its values. In fact, I could almost see him surpassing our father's evil intentions.

What I hadn't known at the time was Andrew, my husband, was Amaryllis's older brother, and he'd been bent on finding and reclaiming her. He'd been away, working to amass enough money to purchase her back if necessary and ensure she'd be able to live her life in freedom and comfort.

Andrew hadn't known I was a Haven child, as we were known. I only ever used my mother's name of Mulligan. After all, I'd been just one more bastard born to Travis Haven. A child without value, except for selling into sexual servitude.

When we moved to Haven Town, everything became known to me and him. Finally, I could take up the cause I'd long wanted to campaign for.

Amaryllis—my "niece of burden", as my father called all the little girls he purchased—was also my sister-in-law. She was the young woman Andrew was determined to see released from the hell she lived in. I promised as soon as I knew that I'd assist, for a sweeter and more obedient girl you'd never find. She alone attended to the distasteful tasks, monitored the food in the house, and ensured everything was spotless.

I will do anything I can to assist. Today I will go talk to my father. I don't hold high hopes this time, but I will do what I can.

Gloriana Mulligan-Coultihan

Chapter One

As I stood on the steps, my stomach wobbled. The day I dreaded most had come. Travis Haven III had finally decided the time was come to "wed" me, and I, Amaryllis Coultihan, had no intentions of allowing that to happen.

He was loud, ugly within, and his spirit meaner than an angry viper who'd just been stepped on. Even worse, he already had four wives pregnant and three who'd just given birth, not to mention the others waiting for his attentions.

"No," I whispered and edged around the table.

His father had bought me from my papa many years before. I'd known all along that Papa couldn't keep me. We were poor. Not church mice poor, because they at least had a roof over their heads. Ours was little more than a holed tin sheet on a ramshackle shed, and food was whatever we could scrounge up day to day.

After the transaction, I'd grown up in the household, learning early what my future would be and shoring up my place. The older I got, the more I'd made a point of becoming indispensable around the house where I now lived, but worked on remaining as invisible as possible. I'd been obedient and quiet, thinking I could simply stay out of sight. Stupidly, I guess, I'd thought if I ensured the household ran smoothly, took over the upkeep of meals and staff, neither man would be interested in me and what I could give them.

I'd had a cursory education too. Master insisted on that.

I could count and read because a "Haven wife" should never be illiterate, or slovenly, I'd been informed regularly. The women they'd taken to "wife" wore delicate gowns and could converse on a wide number of subjects. They were encouraged to read the papers and take an interest in the local society.

Education would uplift them, Master reminded us weekly at the prayer sessions. In truth, it hid how they were treated as little more than concubines and slaves. We really only had one job, and that was to populate the township for these horrible men and their followers.

I'd always known I had too much spirit, but this time, I let it rise.

"You *will* wed me this evening," Travis—Junior, as the younger called himself in the house—screamed across the long refectory-like meal table, and it broke through the reverie.

The wives sat at the lengthy table with round eyes and backs straight as rods while I headed toward the door. Escaping sounded like the only viable prospect right now.

I need to be quick!

Whether I'd reach the door remained to be seen.

A blustering woman rose and sidled up to the door, cutting off my escape route. I stopped and turned as my knees knocked together and fear tied my brain into knots. "Stop right there," she growled.

"No. I will not." My voice shook, and I twisted my hands around. "I won't do it." Very few ever stood up to these big men, and I was truthfully terrified.

Travis advanced and raised a hand. I knew what that meant and ducked, hearing the gasps of those in the dining room. His face was white with fury. He'd moved past scarlet about five minutes ago, and Master, as the older preferred to be called, had risen to stalk to this end of the table.

"You will wed my son, girl, or I'll cut you off," he growled, eyes colder than a midwinter day.

Terror shot through me.

I'd seen what happened to those they cast off. Ignominy and poverty were the first two words to come to mind, but I refused to submit to their kind of life. I'd live in penury if it meant I could escape their version of society.

I wouldn't bear children continuously, fodder for more unhappy "families" of Haven Town. There were too many other bastards to do that to another child. Or to me.

Times had changed here, even against the decree of the Haven family. They might rule the town in 1893, but progress inched on nonetheless. I shook my head, refusing to accede to their will.

"Then leave," Master sneered, and I stepped backward, making sure not to trip over anyone, my gaze frozen on the two men who glowered and snarled like rabid dogs.

"Fine. I'm going."

I scurried quickly, sidling beside the woman, who gaped at me. Reaching out, I turned the knob, and the door to salvation swung open. *Just one more step and I'll be free!*

A voice—Travis's—imperiously called, "Stop right there!"

Years of training and punishment stopped me in my tracks as my fingers clutched at the doorjamb. My heart thudded in my chest, while the clamminess of my hands was unmistakable.

I turned and looked at his face. A cruel smile emerged, though his eyes glittered like shards of ice. "Those clothes aren't yours. They belong to us."

Shock coursed through me. My clothes, the only covering I owned apart from a filthy housedress I wore while undertaking chores, weren't mine?

They would strip me?
They'd leave me naked?
"I..."

Travis reached for me. Now the glare in his eye turned a shining red that told me he would do whatever it took to exact revenge for my refusal.

My hand curled over the knob, and I ran, hurrying out the door. All the while, I attempted to evade his hands. I knew what was hidden beneath the heavy leather gloves. The lights and metal. I'd only ever once before seen him without them, and that was when he'd been "cleaning up after himself", the night Eldora, one of the "wives", had disappeared.

The circuitry in his hands had spun and whizzed, and the sounds of the automaton that worked them had gleamed beneath his skin. Like many of the upper class, he'd had "enhancements" fitted. Master and his son didn't flaunt their additions, but you knew in the way they held themselves, the smirking laughter on their faces, that they welcomed them.

Before her disappearance, Eldora had confided men like Junior used the enhancements for their own pleasure. These two were brutal men who'd made choices that never appeared to end well for those on the receiving end of their threats and interest. No, more than one "wife" had been damaged by their pleasures.

The steps felt so far away as I hurried across the wooden decking, careful lest I slid and fell.

All these memories and the fear coalesced inside my chest.

Strong hands caught me as I scurried for freedom. I fought the touch, but they folded around me. It was a woman I knew by scent.

Gloriana.

Master's daughter.

"What's going on?" Her voice echoed around me, and not for the first time, I'd been grateful for her intervention. She'd done so many times before she'd run away.

"Step away, harlot," Master called.

I felt her still, the sinews and muscles locking tight as if the barb had driven itself deep into her gut. "I am no harlot. I am your daughter, and I intend to talk to you about Amaryllis." She tugged me closer. "Don't move," she murmured.

I was terrified, but Gloriana had never lied or let me down before. In that moment, I had to trust her. My fingers clutched at her, likely even bit deep, but I wasn't letting go. Here was the path to freedom.

"You orchestrated her disobedience?" Master demanded.

I felt her inhale. "I have never orchestrated disobedience. What I did is defend, care for, and show concern for those less fortunate."

"Then take the bitch with you," Junior snarled. "But give us what belongs to us first."

"What?" Confusion coloured the air.

"The clothes. They belong to us." Junior's voice took on a hideously amused tone, and I locked my knees, hoping and pleading inwardly that she wouldn't strip me and add to the current indignity I was captured in.

I cowered in her embrace, fear and hope warring mercilessly in my breast.

"You cannot be serious," Gloriana said, and I heard the horror in her voice. She slid her cape around us both, as if shielding me.

A clawlike hand settled on my shoulder.

I tried to shrug Junior off me, but he dug in, fingers squeezing on my collarbone.

I jerked, but that action didn't work either, as he grasped the material of my shirt and tore it from me.

"Be still!" came an unfamiliar voice. I didn't know it, and yet there was comfort in it. Despite that, I cowered now, because this was a deeply male tone I couldn't place.

"Leave her be, Travis. I'll return the garments later today," Gloriana added as that other voice called, "Leave the girl alone."

Whimpering, I peered over Gloriana's shoulder. There stood a man. He could have been in his late twenties or early thirties with eyes of piercing emerald and a brooding brow. A. shock of dark hair and a savagely jagged scar on his left cheek caught my attention. His shoulders were broad, but it was the badge on his chest that soothed me a little.

Sheriff.

I'd heard of him.

New to town and with a will of iron.

His gaze caught mine, full of concern, before his eyes flicked up to Gloriana. "Take the girl. Bring the clothing to me later today, and I'll return it." There was no mistaking the authority in his tone.

Manly.

I quivered even as my interest rose. Until now, I'd never met a man who could be manly and authoritative without also being hard and ruthless. Yet I saw caring and concern in his gaze. It was confusing and terrifying.

"Come on, Ammy," Gloriana said and steered me toward the

carriage at the foot of the steps. It was black and shiny, horseless as many of the best were. The door opened without a squeak, and I climbed in, Gloriana following me and settling beside me.

My tummy cramped. Not with hunger but with fear.

What will become of me?

On instinct, I turned to look out the window and caught sight of the sheriff climbing the steps. Then the carriage jerked and started moving away from the house on a hiss.

We entered the glade. I knew Gloriana and Andrew lived in a large house outside town, but I certainly didn't expect what met my gaze.

The house was more than the hovel Master had alluded to in his daily "sermons" and classes on the perils of leaving the Haven family, as he called it.

This building was sprawling. It rose from the ground impressively. Three stories of windows and not a shingle in sight. Here was an imposing structure of rock and wood, sheltered from the prying eyes of town by large trees that gave the effect of a wonderland. The driveway was long and imposing, crushed rock crunching beneath the wheels as we rolled forward at a stately pace. The glass shone bright, and flowers bloomed in carefully ordered beds tended by men with scythes.

In the distance, I noted other buildings. "Where are we?" I breathed.

Gloriana took my hand. "This is my home, Amaryllis. Yours too, now. Andrew wanted to come with me, but I held him off. He's been so worried about you."

I knew my brother had wed Gloriana some time back. I'd been informed by Junior in one of his sour moods and had secretly rejoiced that this beautiful woman who'd done so much for the forsaken had found my brother. We'd been poor growing up, but Andrew and I had been close once. Then I'd been passed to Master. After, when Papa's money came in, my father had made approaches to bring me home. I wouldn't have known, except I'd been in the front room one day when he saw Master. All those overtures had been ignored, and I'd lost hope that I'd ever be free.

Until today.

"But what will I do?" I leaned a little closer to the glass, peering through the gathering gloom.

"First, you'll heal."

I turned to the woman beside me and frowned. "Heal?"

"Yes." She nodded. "You've lived a long time in captivity. I doubt anyone has cared for you since you arrived there, and you need time to find who and what you are. Then you'll need to decide what and who you want to be."

Such an odd concept, I thought, but nodded and waited for the carriage to stop under a portico.

The door opened, and out strode a man. He wasn't the boy I remembered with gangly arms and legs. No, instead he was strong and muscular, his eyes piercing first me, then Gloriana. "You've got her." A wealth of relief echoed in his voice.

I clenched my hands because I wanted to run and hug him, but years of training restrained me. Would he bully me into doing his will? Require me to marry immediately? It occurred to me that I no longer knew my brother.

So many questions and fears crowded in. Perhaps this was what Gloriana spoke of?

"And just in time too. Let's go inside and find some food and a bath for Amaryllis. Then we can talk."

I didn't dare speak to Gloriana's answer; I didn't know what was expected of me or allowed in this fine household.

I allowed myself to be ushered inside, and there in the hall, a group of people waited. The female staff were dressed in blue cotton gowns with overlong white aprons, the men in breeches and white shirts with vests. I turned and watched as Gloriana tugged her hatpin free, then removed her hat. Her red hair glinted under the lights, and I felt dirty and unworthy to stand before her. An interloper.

Andrew came close, his face tight, eyes betraying his concern as I tensed when he reached out. "I'm glad you're here, Ammy."

My eyes pricked with hot tears. It had been years since any family member called me that. I nodded and ducked my head, and he kept his distance, as if he understood I was wary of a male's touch.

"I'll take her upstairs, find some clothes, and Ammy can bathe. If you could arrange for a meal to be prepared in the parlour, then we can talk." Gloriana spoke over my head, and her words further discommoded me.

With a gentle hand, she steered me toward the steps and up them. My feet made no sound as I stepped up the deeply carpeted treads to the top. Then she ushered me to the right. The hallway was a dark cherry-wood-panelled walk, but lights lit the way. No candles here, unlike at the much older Haven House. Only Master's and Junior's rooms were furnished richly, apart from the main living areas; they claimed it was because they required it for their work, but I knew better. They had kept us in the dark because it also ensured we remained cowed.

I faltered, wondering just how much money Andrew had now as I noted the marble tables that sat between doorways and the heavy scent of roses and lilies.

"I'm..." What was I trying to say? I couldn't stay here? Felt uncomfortable?

"It's okay," Gloriana offered, then opened a door into a luxurious room.

"Your room?" I asked, and she shook her head.

"This one is all yours. Let's organise a bath, and I'll see what clothing I have on hand that may fit you."

Gloriana had a slender figure but was taller and with a bust I could only hope for.

As I turned to thank her for the kindness of a roof over my head and clothing on my body, I realised she'd already left.

I'd never entered a room like this before. I'd been in both Junior's and Master's rooms, but only to oversee the cleaning and the redecoration when they required it. There had been heavy sconces lining the walls with electric lighting, not that I'd ever seen it on. The only light that ever entered those rooms was through windows covered with heavy drapes and shutters.

It was totally unlike the rooms most of the women lived in, which were long and narrow, lined with double bunks and a row of shared trunks in the middle for clothing. At the end of the room were the ablution stands, with sinks and three long mirrors. Once they were pregnant or had children, they took a two-bedroom suite, featuring a room for the young children and their carer while the mother had a private room. They were small, with room for a narrow bed and crib only and mostly without a window, but the privacy was worth so much to my mind. Only the favoured got windows looking out onto the lawns.

I jerked into motion, stepping forward and brushing aside the heavy velvet drapes. Beyond lay the forest, a sea of green with the sparkle of the mountain stream in the distance.

My guts lurched. This was so alien to anything I knew.

"I can't—" The contents of my stomach rose to my throat, burning their way up.

The door opened, and a woman, not much older than me, entered. "I'm Evie. Miss Gloriana sent me with clothing for you." In her arms lay piles of gowns and skirts, undergarments, and shoes.

She bustled in and settled the pile on the floor, but not before I heard the telltale *whir-whizz* sound. I turned. "You're an automaton?"

Her lips turned up. "Yes. Fully integrated single leg after amputation at four. Why?"

In the past, we'd been told automaton implantation was only for the rich and powerful. We'd been starved of such technological improvements in Haven Town, and this young woman was telling me that everything I understood was a lie.

"I... uh..." Embarrassment flooded through me. "I'm sorry. I should have..."

She waved my hand away. "Miss Gloriana explained your background to me. Said it would be good for you to meet me so you'd learn about the greater world. Now let me help you bathe. Then I'm to show you downstairs to Master Andrew's study. They're organising a light meal for the three of you tonight."

Before I knew it, I'd been assisted out of the torn gown. The tub, hidden behind a large screen, bubbled with scented water, and I immersed myself quickly, figuratively scrubbing away years of servitude and poverty. As hard as I scrubbed, though, the memories stuck tight. Tears burned in my eyes, but I wouldn't let them fall.

Evie returned just as the water was starting to cool. "Those clothes are being sent back to that place. Now, here's a nice thick towel to dry yourself with."

Rising from the water, I felt the material envelop me. It smelled of lavender and something else, and I took it without a word, rubbing myself dry as I tried to sort through the surprise I felt at the softness of it. In the past, all I'd known was rough and hard-wearing.

Then Evie thrust a chemise at me, and I tugged it on, followed by the rest of the clothing. She helped with buttons at the back of the gown and placed a pair of slippers on the floor. I slid them on and let her tug a brush through my hair. Every stroke was soothing.

Looking into the mirror, I realised, not for the first time, that my life had changed. Whether it was for the good, I couldn't possibly work out yet.

She tucked my hair into a tidy knot, and I rose, following her to the door. "They prefer to eat early. More often in the summer, they'll take their dinner outside on the terrace, but tonight they wanted to make sure you'd be comfortable," Evie explained.

Comfortable. A strange word choice given the circumstances I currently found myself in.

I stopped just inside Andrew's study, his back to me as I entered. Gloriana rose from the small table laid with plates, glasses, and cutlery.

He must have heard the door close behind me, because he turned, gaze wary as he looked at me. "Ammy, I wish we could have released you earlier."

The name he used, both familiar and yet not, filled me with a quivering sensation. One that spoke of fear and hopefulness in equal measure.

"I..." What was there to say? I couldn't have saved myself, given the way all the girls were watched and kept indoors.

Gloriana shushed him, and we settled at the table. We'd regularly sat with Master, yet I felt at sea. They passed the potatoes and the meats, which smelled delicious. I loved the taste of fowl, though it was rarely served in Haven House. Tonight, the chicken was succulent and served in a creamy sauce. It coated my tongue and tanged a little like citrus before sliding down with almost no effort.

Andrew remained silent, as did I, and Gloriana soon gave up her attempts at chatter.

Glasses clinked and metal clanked on the china dishes as I ate.

By the time the meal was done, I wanted out of the room and away. Solitude had long been my friend, and I anxiously sought it.

As I rose to clear the dishes, Gloriana reached out. "No, that's Amelia's task."

The girl who'd slipped within the room moments before stepped up and removed the plates. I remained still, unsure of what to do next.

Once the table was cleared, Gloriana took my arm, and I followed her, aware that Andrew trailed behind. "We should retire to the salon," Gloriana cooed.

The room was spacious and decorated in bright colours of yellow, pink, and light green. The walls were covered with paper that carried sprigs of flowers. In the middle, on a large mat, sat several chairs. The chaise and several armchairs gathered around a squat table. I settled into the single as Gloriana sat on the chaise and Andrew in the armchair beside me.

"Why?" The word slid from my lips, even though I had tried valiantly to stop just that happening. "Why now?"

Andrew sighed. "I made representations before, Ammy." His eyes were wild, as if he'd spent years dealing with pain. He dragged unsteady fingers through his hair, and I watched in surprise.

"The Haven sect is not welcoming of families once a child has been handed over. We, Father and I, offered him more than he paid for you, but he refused to release you. It didn't matter what we said. We even attempted the local judge, but he refused. Said we'd given up all rights to you. We *tried*, Ammy."

My stomach knotted at the agony in his voice. What could I say or do to relieve him of this? No words came to me, so I let him talk.

"Gloriana here, she knew what you were going through. She had a friend, someone within the household who'd monitored you. They warned us that this was coming."

An informant. I'd be willing to bet Master and Junior would give their eyeteeth to know who. I'd as soon keep that information under wraps, though. Neither of the men was what you'd call welcoming or accepting of other ideas, and I didn't owe them any loyalty. I'd only done what was needed to survive.

"I don't know what you want me to say." I honestly didn't. I could prevaricate, but that would be counterproductive. I wanted to feel some affinity with my brother. I'd yearned for a familial connection. Not that I held what they did against them. We'd been poor. Unable to even pay for the most basic necessities. They'd honestly sought to give me a chance at a life, but no matter how you coated it, the truth was the same.

I'd been a slave until they'd decided I'd be good enough to become an incubator for their twisted beliefs.

A shaft of frigid hate slashed at me. Not at Andrew or Gloriana, but at the men who made up the Haven community.

"I would like to go to bed now." I kept my voice even because I was struggling to hold in the violent emotions that threatened to overwhelm me.

I saw Andrew glance at Gloriana, saw the wince she gave him back, but I couldn't hold on any longer. Over ten years of suffering couldn't be eased this quickly.

I rose. "Please." It wasn't a request.

Gloriana rose and shook a tiny bell. Evie, the servant who'd helped me dress, entered the room. "Ma'am?"

"Miss Amaryllis is ready to retire." Gloriana smiled, though it barely reached her eyes, and I grunted inwardly.

"Thank you," I added, more than aware that I hadn't acted exactly like the perfect... whatever I was.

I followed Evie out and up the steps. Questions crowded my mind, but none of them had answers I was likely ready to hear, so I ignored them and kept walking up the steps and to the bedroom.

"This is the switch for the lights, Miss Amaryllis." She showed me the little brown lever, and I nodded with thanks, noting the clean white nightgown waiting on the bed. Without another word, she unbuttoned the back of the gown I was wearing. I slipped out of it, tugged the light chemise over my head, and released the pins from my hair under Evie's careful watch.

"If there's nothing else, miss?"

I shook my head. "No. Thank you, Evie."

Suddenly, I couldn't get rid of her quickly enough; the tension inside me was ready to explode. Emotions that threatened to suffocate me if I didn't give them the release they demanded.

As if she knew, the girl bobbed a curtsy and left me in the room.

Just like that, the sobs tore out of me as if I'd popped the cork on a bottle.

I sank to the floor, hand in mouth, and bit down, because no one must hear me cry. I learned that very early in the "care" of Haven House.

When the terrible storm passed, I lay there, exhausted, until my eyes closed and sleep claimed me.

Chapter Two

I'd been here four days. Long, dragging days of sitting around while Gloriana tried to arrange clothing for me, introduced me to the household, but refused to allow me to assist in the daily duties. Unused as I was to leisure, I wandered the gardens, aware I was watched the whole time by gardeners, servants, and even Gloriana and Andrew. On a purely unemotional level, I understood their fear that I might disappear. It occurred to me as a way of escaping the bubble of loss that surrounded me.

It was hard to explain the intensities of highs and lows to someone who hadn't experienced and lived as I had.

Gloriana had been born into it, had escaped of her own free will. I had been bought and paid for.

Just this morning, Evie had passed on intelligence that curdled my stomach.

"Miss Gloriana and Master Andrew returned from Haven House late last night." She'd been placing my clothing into the drawers, and I'd sat on the bed, watching. I wasn't even allowed to assist with this most basic of tasks.

"Why were they there?"

"Returning what they said wasn't theirs. James, the driver, said they took a small bag of coins. Making rapara... Repair..."

"Reparation," I added.

Evie nodded. "Something like that, yes."

I grunted. So, they'd paid back the silver coins that had exchanged hands. Returned the shredded gown. I wanted to tell Evie I'd pay them back, but with what? I'd stewed all morning over the knowledge of what had occurred. I was still a commodity.

This afternoon, at lunch, Gloriana set me a task. One that seemed utterly pointless to my mind, but it was all she'd asked of me, so I would repay the kindnesses she'd shown me.

The paints and brushes lay before me. "So, what now?" Peering at the blank canvas, I was sure it mocked me. The dark colours—greys, browns, and blacks—echoed my state of mind.

No one responded.

I'd painted as a young girl. It was one of the few things that had brought me joy before I'd been surrendered to that house of horrors, but years had passed since then.

On a whim, I dipped the brush into the black and slashed at the canvas, then added yellow and red, then rocked back on my heels.

No, I couldn't see anything in it. No joy. Nothing. Just muddy, dark colours.

The urge to throw my brush at the canvas called. A dark urge I would overcome.

I'd never been an angry person until now.

Tears of fury and frustration bubbled over, and I turned, looking to see who watched me from the house or the gardens.

No one.

Am I brave enough?

I slid the brush back into the holder, remaining calm, in case anyone was watching me. Then, inhaling deeply, I took the first step, moving across the grass.

Step. Step. Step.

Not looking around. Making it seem as if I knew what I was doing with no rush. When I got to the edge of the woods, I reached out, ready to push aside a branch.

"Going somewhere?"

A deep, dark voice, reminiscent of chocolate and something more inviting, slid over me like a glove. I turned and gasped when I saw who stood there.

"What...?"

The sheriff watched me, his long dark hair glinting in the sunlight while the verdant green of his eyes reflected on me. Like a deep pond, I wanted to fall into them.

He cleared his throat. "Mrs. Coultihan asked me to bring you in. She wanted to talk to you about something." The trill of his accent, southern and drugging, captured me.

I needed a moment to throw off the confusion that filled my brain. "I..."

At Haven House, we'd been warned such men as this were dangerous. They'd take our chastity, use us, and throw us away when they were done. Yet for all the danger in the broad set of his shoulders and the slashing of his heavily stubbled chin, there was no thrum of alarm running through me. I wondered in that moment if this was another of their controlling mantras. The only men who'd scared me in my time at Haven House had been Junior and Master. No other men were allowed into the house proper. I'd need to think about that.

"Come," he said.

He reached out a gloved hand, and I took it, glancing quickly over my shoulder to the forest behind me. I'd wasted my opportunity to run, so I walked beside him.

"You've had time to settle in here now." He said it more like a statement, and I glanced at him.

"Not really. I mean, I don't have a purpose or some way to fill my days." The urge to curse my unruly mouth was a heavy weight.

"It'll come."

We reached the flagged steps, and he urged me up and took the treads one at a time, stepping sideways in an ungainly fashion.

"Are you okay?" The words just slipped out.

He grimaced. "Fine. Getting over an accident."

At the door, he stopped. "I'll follow you in a moment, Miss Amaryllis." He tipped his hat, turned, and headed for the young groundskeeper who strode into view.

I pushed the strange conversation from my brain as I entered the house.

"So, as you can see, Miss Amaryllis, if you wish to be of assistance to these ladies, then you will need to start by going out and meeting with them." Delilah Simmonds sat on the edge of her seat, nodding at her own plan.

Of course, I wanted to help the others who'd left Haven House and the horrible church they claimed was "God's Will on Earth", but fright held me tight in its fist. In the week since the sheriff's visit—and I still didn't know why he'd been here—I'd spoken with Gloriana about my future. Neither she nor Andrew saw any reason for me to change, but I wasn't a girl to whom sitting still came easily.

We'd discussed my painting, what I wanted to achieve with my life, but I'd kept so much in. The one thing Gloriana had pressed on me was a journal this morning. *"Keep it with you, dear. When you're ready to plan your future, this might be the first step in sharing it."*

The tiny book resided in my pocket right now, and I surreptitiously patted it.

Gloriana touched my knee lightly, bringing me back to the matter at hand and the women who'd gathered in the parlour. I'd lost track of the conversation and now knew all eyes rested on me.

"Uh, forgive me, Mrs Simmonds. I was not attending fully." I hated to admit I had no clue what they needed from me because I'd been lost in my own thoughts.

"I was saying to your dear sister Gloriana that we could begin the visits tomorrow. Letitia Hemingswood is in a bad way, so very sick, and the future looks grim for her. Her children will be lost without her. You could visit with her, maybe take her a basket. That would be an ideal introduction to the women who've left Haven."

Letitia. The name didn't ring any bells for me, but that meant little. She may have been one of the other scion's wives.

I glanced at Gloriana, well aware that I would need guidance and help. She nodded her assent, though her gaze was thoughtful as it rested on me.

"Yes, of course," I answered and then gave my attention to Mrs Simmonds once more.

"Good," she cooed, rising. "Let me know how you get along, Ms Coultihan." She extended her hand, and I shook it, still very much at sea in the situation. Then I trailed Gloriana to the door.

Once Evie shut it behind the woman and her entourage, I turned to Gloriana. "I don't understand." I moved back into the room, settling into one of the deep armchairs.

"It's a long story," she answered, rubbing the tip of her finger over the creases that appeared on her brow. "Letitia was Reverend Cunningham's last wife. I know much of the story from word of mouth, but I believe it to be reliable. She was very young and innocent at the time of their wedding. When the reverend passed on, his many wives were parcelled out like gifts. Some to his sons and others to men of the church. Only Junior and Master didn't take any on. Letitia was given to the oldest man in the church, a man they considered to be *worthy*. He beat the children, particularly Letitia's oldest child, and her because he said they were wicked. Letitia ran away with help from non-believers is what I understand. You didn't hear about this?"

I shook my head. "After you left, we were refused outside society, except the matrons and wives who were deemed *worthy*."

Gloriana's countenance took on a thoughtful cast, as if she were considering what role she played in the drama of my life.

"Daughters and the unwed were kept far away. All we knew was what the wives told us as we went about our chores."

Gloriana nodded. "Tomorrow, you and I will call on Letitia. It's been some time since I visited with her. The children, by the sounds of it, will need some consideration if she is indeed as ill as Mrs Simmonds suggests."

"Of course." I expected to be dismissed, but Gloriana continued to study me. "Is something amiss?"

"No, dear. Just... I know you're not happy. Is there anything I can do to assist?"

I started at her query, nerves jumping just below the skin. "I'm not unhappy..." My voice petered away.

Gloriana's eyes widened with surprise, but she kept quiet while I thought about how to continue.

My hands were clasped in my lap, and I held them tight, hoping not to betray my unease further. "I don't know what you and Andrew expect of me." I couldn't help the lost tone from emerging and shrugged. "I'm here surrounded by this lovely... I don't know what you want of me. I'm happy to clean, to cook, or anything. Just let me be useful." The words tumbled free, and much as I may wish to call them back, there was no way to do so.

Gloriana sighed and slumped farther down in her seat. "I know how you feel, but things are different in normal society. You're the sister of the master of this house. You're not supposed to work—"

I opened my mouth, but she stayed me with a raised hand.

"I understand, Amaryllis." She nodded. "We were raised to believe a woman must be useful to the house in which she lives before marriage. To contribute to the overall good of those around us and their comfort. To prove our worthiness for marriage with assistance, expecting nothing back."

These words were the mantra I'd grown up by in that horrible house. Words that bit like acid deep into my brain. They may as well have been engraved into my skin, because they were words I'd abided by for so long.

She reached toward me, entreating me to listen. "We can find a way forward, Ammy. One that suits both your needs and your new position."

"But what?" I couldn't control the sudden need that bloomed in my chest. I needed to be useful, not for marriage or any other subservient will of the men of Haven but for me. To at least feel that I'd regained a bit of my personal identity.

Gloriana moved so she now crouched on the floor in front of me. It was an incongruous sight, this woman, self-assured and immaculately dressed before me. "We start by showing others that the way of Haven is wrong. That we are worth more than simply to breed their next generation."

I wanted that so badly that I shook with the intensity. I clasped my hands together, trying to keep my body from vibrating. "I want to be useful."

She nodded. "Yes. So the first step is to dress you for the role you're going to fulfil."

"Dress me?"

Gloriana's eyes glowed with something akin to unholy glee.

"Yes. We show them that there are ways to be useful, not to be downtrodden. We dress you appropriately to your new status. We go out instead of cowering here like fragile glass. We take control."

Oh my. Those were indeed fighting words.

"But what's wrong with what I'm wearing now?"

Gloriana smiled. "Nothing, but they're mine. You have a style of your own, and we'll show them we are unafraid to be individual."

"How?"

"The dressmaker will be here soon, Amaryllis. We outfit you—"

I shook my head. "The cost—"

"Leave that to me. We won't order more than you're comfortable with, but you will need at least a full range of clothing. Day gowns, visiting gowns, and evening wear."

Shock filled me at her words. "I've never owned..." I gulped. "It's too much."

She shook her head. "No. These are the basic and minimal needs of a woman in our world. The world you now inhabit. Let me guide you."

A step into the unknown if I took it, but one that would give me my place in a society I didn't know. "Fine, then. But promise me I won't be expected to marry without making my own choices."

"Your brother and I would never do that. If and when you're ready, you make your own choices."

I nodded. "Then I accept."

Gloriana exhaled. "Excellent. Mrs Maycroft will be here soon to measure you and take on the ordering of your new wardrobe. Once that is arranged, we can order shoes and boots, wraps, gloves, and hats." She rose and headed to the sideboard. "Have a cup of tea with me before we prepare."

I let her pour and accepted the cup she offered while silently considering what I'd agreed to and wondering what would come next.

Did I make the right decision?

Only time would tell, but it didn't stop the sudden knotting in my belly.

Chapter Three

I looked at the boxes of clothing that were carted into what had become my bedroom. Shoes and various accoutrements seemed to cover every chair and side, while mounds of gowns, wraps, nightwear, and even fine underthings hid the bed from view.

"Do I really need all this?" I whirled to face Gloriana, and she smiled.

"Yes. This is just the start, my dear. She could rework clothing already in her workshop to arrange for an overnight delivery, and the shops had some of the other items we needed. Now, let's see. Perhaps the violet walking gown with the white boots. You'll need a matching cloak and gloves. I'll send Evie along to assist you to dress and attend to your hair." There was laughter in Gloriana's words and a grin on her face.

"But you said—"

The grin fled, and the mirth was replaced with a serious look. "This is nothing compared to what many of the more well-to-do ladies have, Amaryllis."

So much stuff! I gazed back at the piles and found it hard to explain why I felt so discomforted with more than I'd ever had. Then I realised. I was out of my depth. Of course, Gloriana understood. She'd grown up in the same household. So why was I struggling when clearly she didn't? "How did you manage it?"

Gloriana touched my cheek. "How did I manage what?"

"Come to be comfortable like this? With everything you need and more on hand."

She sighed and took my hand. "It takes lots of time, Ammy."

I clearly had no compass. "I don't understand," I whispered.

"I know" was her response before she left me there in the room alone.

The woman standing before me was one I didn't know. Hair piled on top of my head, fastened with large metal combs, the gown hugging my body, so every aspect of my form was emphasised. Previously, the gowns I'd worn had been cinched in with a sash, ensuring the fit, while the bust was hit or miss, depending on which item of clothing was allocated to me daily.

My shoes hugged my feet, but there was no sagging at the toe or heel, and they were new. Fitted for me.

Evie returned and clasped the cloak around my shoulders. "Well, Miss Amaryllis, you look very nice indeed."

My eyes shone, emphasising the violet tinge, and when I accepted the tiny bag Evie thrust into my hands, I felt like another woman.

"I still can't believe this is me."

She grinned, and I returned it with a shy smile.

"We should go down now. Miss Gloriana said she'll wait, and they've ordered the horseless carriage for you both."

Horseless carriages. I knew Master and Junior had one, the invention making the most of the new steam-powered electric system, and I'd ridden in one during the fraught trip here, but apart from that, I'd never been in one.

"Why don't they have horses?"

Evie smiled. "They do, but for these visits, Miss Gloriana prefers the horseless carriage. I think it's so she can make a statement to the likes of her father and brother." As if horrified, the maid slid her fingers over her mouth, eyes wide with remorse. "Oh, I'm sorry. I didn't mean to—"

I waved her concerns aside. I could well understand Gloriana's thinking. She could and had made a good life for herself despite the stones her family had tossed at her. "I knew what you meant, and I take no offence. We should go down now." I smiled at the maid. "Will you be accompanying us?"

Evie shook her head, face still a hot red blush. "No, miss." She ducked her head as I exited the room.

At the bottom of the stairs waited Gloriana. She smiled and nodded as I descended the stairs. "Beautiful. Just as I hoped." When I reached her, she took my hand and wound her arm around mine, so we were side by side and arm in arm. It was odd. I felt strangely pleased with her action. My experience left me wondering why I felt this way.

She tugged me through the door, and I stepped up in the carriage after her. The door closed us inside, while the coachman sat in a tiny stall at the front.

This time, I listened as we drove. It chugged and whirred, the wheels rolling down the drive and crunching on the stone. The gates clanged shut behind us, but not before I got a look at the inside of the gate-house. Large rods and wheels turned.

"Is that where the electricity for the house is generated?" I wondered aloud.

Gloriana shook her head. "No. It merely powers the gates and the security systems."

I blinked. "Security systems?"

"Yes. On that note, you must never venture outside at night without checking with Andrew or myself. We have automative dogs patrolling. The human handlers working with them carry tiny devices that allow them to deactivate them should the need arise, but Andrew assures me they bite just like a real dog."

I leaned back into the squabs. Automative dogs, electric lighting, and a steam-driven electric carriage. All things I knew nothing about. "Andrew... he's rich. How did he make so much money?"

Gloriana smiled. "He's particularly clever with automatives. In fact, he designed our security dogs and several other automative things, including carriages. The royalties from his work paid for the house, staff, and everything else you see. He's got several other patents pending. You should ask him about them over dinner."

I turned and looked out the window, amazed that we were almost in Haven's township. It hadn't changed, and that seemed the most amazing fact of all, given the way my life had since I'd been whisked away some ten weeks or so ago.

We drew close to the house where I'd lived for so many years. An imposing three-storey structure plonked down on the highest point in town. Some years ago, during one of the praise sessions Master headed, he'd told the story of them building the major portion.

"And so, after travelling here for so long, my father noted Haven. A perfect place for the settlement of our people. The green hill close to a water supply and much flat land. Here we set down our roots. Here we planted the seeds of Haven, and here we will remain until the coming Rapture."

Master surveyed his domain, the florid colour in his cheeks betraying either his excitement or the various glasses he'd quaffed. Which one took precedence over the other, I couldn't say. He raised his glass. "To one and all who embraces Haven and her ways, the doors of Restoration shall open to thee!"

As one, the body had answered with fervent "Amens."

Thinking back now, I couldn't believe anyone actually accepted the words he'd professed to abide by. *Maybe I'm questioning it because I never truly believed?*

The carriage slowed its stately roll and came to a stop outside a small broken-down haberdashery store. The walk was tilting, and the roofing appeared not just flimsy but broken and ready to fly away on the next gust of wind.

"Here we are, Ammy, dear." Before the driver could let himself out, Gloriana had the door open and was climbing down.

I followed her, noting the small faces pressed against the dirty glass. "This is...?"

"Yes." She nodded. "I tried to find her a house and settle her medical bills, but she's proud."

It occurred to me that Letitia Hemingswood had little *but* her pride left if this was where she lived. Gloriana picked her way along the boards, some broken and others rotted, holes appearing so one needed to be careful where they stepped.

Before we knocked on the door, it swung wide, held by a woman in her late twenties. Her hair, sparse as it was, was striped with silver, her frame little more than a skeleton. "Mrs Coultihan, it's a pleasure."

Once invited within, the children gathered around as Gloriana met each by name. "Now, Francesca, I have chalk and boards for you, as well as some books. If you'll settle your sisters and brothers by the fire, I'll pass some time with your mother and Amaryllis."

The oldest child, a girl of maybe thirteen or fourteen, looked at her with dull eyes but accepted the gift in silence.

"She still doesn't speak?" Gloriana enquired of Ms. Hemingswood, who sighed.

"She does when it's family or someone she trusts, but there are so few."

I glanced over my shoulder at the child who'd gathered the others near. "Why isn't she in school?"

Ms. Hemingswood stared at me. "You're new to Haven?"

I shook my head. "No, I've been here since I was young. Master at Haven House—"

Gloriana placed her hand on mine. "Letitia tried to enrol Francesca, but the school was controlled by the church. They refused to accept a 'fallen child' within the congregation, so she homeschools them."

I bit my lip. Though I'd lived in this town almost my entire life, I hadn't truly seen the underbelly of it. I was just now coming to understand that for all my fear and hatred, I'd been sheltered from the very worst.

"I'm sorry, Ms. Hemingswood."

She nodded. "I'm not worried for me but for the children. They don't deserve to be ostracised because of their birthplace and the father." She wiped her face, which was suddenly bathed in sweat. She slumped, hand to her chest, and the oldest child, Francesca, set the younger ones aside and hurried to her side.

"Mama?" There was a wealth of fear in her voice, the way it cracked on the last syllable almost too much for me to bear.

"I'm fine. Just a little turn." She straightened, though her lips appeared bloodless and her face told of the strain. "Go back to the little ones, dear."

Gloriana passed the woman the cup from the table beside her.

Letitia took a sip, wiped her face with a handkerchief she'd retrieved from her pocket, and glanced at Gloriana. "Mrs Simmonds told me of your offer. It's most gracious, but—"

Gloriana shook her head. "No. But it will keep your children together, housed, and will assure their education. Please accept this offer."

I couldn't help but wonder what it was, but decided it would be best to wait until I had Gloriana's total attention in the carriage.

"I couldn't..." Letitia whispered.

"For the children," Gloriana urged.

"But who will escort them?" She teared up, and my heart practically broke for the woman.

"One of our family. If not myself, then my husband or his sister, Amaryllis." She waved in my direction.

I started upon hearing Gloriana use my name.

"The sheriff will also accompany them," Gloriana whispered.

The woman's shoulders slumped. "When?"

"Only when you're ready. But there is paperwork. Guardianship agreements and so on. It must be ironclad to protect the children."

It all sounded so cloak-and-dagger, but I realised if what I guessed was happening was correct, then she clearly feared for the safety of the children. I had a lot to ask Gloriana about on the way home.

A sheaf of papers was withdrawn from the bottom of the large basket Gloriana had carried in. She presented them to Letitia and explained what they meant. With a shaking hand, the woman signed every page. Then I acted as a witness.

"They will be safe, Letitia. I will ensure it," Gloriana vowed as we took our leave soon after.

We climbed back into the carriage, but not before I caught sight of another standing on the corner watching us. Junior.

Once safely within, I told Gloriana, who frowned. "You're sure?"

"Yes. Now please explain. What are you doing with the children? I assume from the paperwork that you plan to remove them and send them away when Letitia passes on?"

With lips tight, Gloriana nodded. "We discovered early on, of the women who were ostracised, the church usually swept in and removed the children. In the beginning, we had no legal instrument to fight the church. After we lost several children, we realised there must be an agreement. Since then, Andrew ensured we had a lawyer we could call upon. He drafts the guardianship papers, which we then send to the governor. Only once did Master try to overturn them. We beat him, and he now knows we mean business."

I bit my lip. "You want me to accompany them."

There wasn't an answer, simply a long look, which curdled my insides.

"What?" I questioned.

"I cannot, Amaryllis. Not now. I must limit for some time the amount of travelling I undertake. On doctor's orders."

"You're ill?" I leaned forward and took her hand.

"No. Not exactly. Only increasing."

"Oh..." Stupid thing to say, but no other words crossed my mind.

"It's all right, Amaryllis. We have been hoping and praying for this miracle. But it makes it harder to attend to my ladies."

"I see. I would be happy to accompany them, but do I need the sheriff?" My fingers suddenly became quite interesting as I looked down. The tall, long-haired man had a barely contained humanity to him, and I wasn't sure time in his company would be easy.

Gloriana laughed. "Yes." But then the smile died away. "A lone woman travelling with children is a target. With a man, and furthermore one with a badge? You will be as safe as we can make you."

"On the train, then."

Now her smile returned. "Of course not. We'll use a dirigible."

"A what?" This was a word I'd never heard before.

"You'll learn." Gloriana's eyes fairly danced with laughter. "Later."

Later. The word my life revolved around.

Dinner was sombre. Andrew arrived home, and he closeted himself in his office until Gloriana knocked on it and disappeared within. When they both exited the room, her face was red and blotchy, his lips set in a line of pure anger.

I took my seat at the small round table and ate in silence. The food was delicious, but my stomach knotted, wondering what might have upset them both so much. Once the meal was done, dishes tidied away, Andrew stood and closed the doors to the room.

I sat stock-still.

He took his place at the table. "Junior has an agreement signed by our father. It says there is no way you can be released from their custody." He gazed at me, long and hard. "I won't send you back there, but anything less is illegal, according to his lawyers. I can and will fight it. Eventually I'll win, because ownership of another being under our constitution is neither binding nor legal."

Bile rose in my throat. Junior thought he owned me. *He'll make me marry him...*

I dashed from the room, heading for the nearest bathroom, and threw up, sour spittle coating my tongue as I gripped the marble. "Noooo..." But looking at my reflection, I knew everything Andrew said was probably true.

"I don't want to go back to him." Even as I mumbled the words, my brain was forming ideas.

I could flee.

You have no money, no contacts, and nowhere to go, my brain unhelpfully countered.

A gentle rapping sound intruded on the fraught moment.

I wiped my face. "Coming," I croaked, then turned and opened the door. Gloriana stood there, sorrow heavy on her face.

"Andrew and the sheriff are here. You should come back to the dining room." She took my hand and led me like a child to the room I'd left in a hurry mere moments before.

I took my place at the table and noted the grim look on the sheriff's face. "Miss Amaryllis, I'm so sorry to hear the news." He glanced at Andrew, as if seeking his guidance.

Andrew nodded. "You should tell her everything, Damien."

The man sighed, scooped up the drink that Evie had delivered, and took a sip of the wine. "I am Damien Whitmore. I'm an agent for the Presidential Rescue of Innocents Endangered by Spirituality Task Force. We are known as agents of PRIEST."

I stared at the man, not for the first time surprised by him, his presence, or what he spoke of.

"I was sent here to investigate the Haven Church, or sect, as your brother Andrew rightly titles it. My job is to infiltrate, gather data, and ensure the safety of anyone considered 'at-risk.'"

He inhaled, and I watched the flare of his nostrils, the way his hands clenched on the table, as if every tiny aspect of him were vitally important to my continued survival.

"Miss Amaryllis, your brother contacted me tonight when he received this missive. I've read it, and your safety is paramount to..." He stilled for a moment. "I can remove you from this situation while my men come in and deal with it, but that leaves Letitia Hemingswood's children without support."

In his eyes, I read pain. "I'm willing to go back—" My voice broke as I stood. "I will go back if it ensures everyone else's safety." I would. Because anything less than helping would be akin to saying this was okay. I knew what I'd be going back to, but I accepted it. As if in sympathy, my body ached like I'd been physically struck. "Just... when it's over, get me back, okay?"

Gloriana sobbed in silence into a white handkerchief, and Damien Whitmore's face turned thunderous. "No. That is not acceptable."

Andrew shook his head. "I agree. This will not happen. I forbid it!"

Heat seared the skin of my face, and tears dribbled down my cheeks. "If it's the only way—"

"No, Miss Amaryllis. We need to hold out just long enough for Letitia to send her children. I have a plan."

"What?" I barely breathed the word as a tiny seed of hope took root. I took a deep drink from my glass, though I grimaced at the bitterness on my tongue.

"Andrew has agreed to send you to the governor. He owes your brother a debt, I believe. We get you there, and I stay with you. Rafe Sargeant, my second, will remain behind and assume duties until Letitia is ready to send the children. I'll send a replacement back. We'll claim we're running off together. I have contacts and places we can stay. We just need to hold out until PRIEST brings charges against Haven."

It was all too much. I rose, my head spinning. "I don't..." The world greyed at the edges. "I feel..."

The ground rushed up to meet me. Before my eyes closed, I heard, "forgive me, Ammy."

Chapter Four

I opened my eyes, the sensation of grogginess and weight warring with the movement. "What's...?"

"Be still" came a voice. One I knew.

Sheriff Whitmore.

"Where am I?" I sat up, though I still felt a little woozy.

"On your brother's dirigible." His voice sounded deeper, tense.

"What?" I threw off the last vestiges of physical unsteadiness and pushed to my feet, noting the small room decorated more like a boudoir. The chaise I'd been lying on was pink and cream, elaborately carved, and matched the two armchairs nearby. I looked ahead, noted a window, and rushed toward it.

When I reached it, I nearly threw up and backed away. "We're in the air!" I squeaked out.

I whirled, and he steadied me, capturing my fluttering hands and drawing me close.

He smelled of sandalwood and horse leather.

He felt hard, like a granite boulder. Hard and immovable.

He radiated heat and something else that left me feeling weak and needy.

I scrunched my eyes shut. "Where are we going? What have you done?"

He laughed a little, the rumble echoing through his body, and I felt frissons of a strange sensation in my nerves. "We are indeed in the air. The dirigible, *Pride of Coultihan*, is taking us to the governor of Scottsvale. With Andrew's permission, I'm removing you from Haven until the agents can do their work."

My nerves quivered and jumped, which was somehow telegraphed to the sheriff.

"Before you ask, your brother and his wife are safely at home." He smiled at me.

In response, a slow curl of heat formed in my belly. Through my confusion, I recognised this was something out of the ordinary and broke away. "I think... Is there some way to perhaps get some tea?" *What's wrong with my voice? It sounds downright shaky!*

His smile melted me further. "Of course. If you just pull the bell, a server will be in."

I scooted away and grabbed the pull. Within a moment, the door opened, and a young man edged inside. "Ms. Coultihan, I'm pleased to see you're feeling better. How may I assist you?"

"Could we have a pot of tea and two cups?"

He smiled. "Of course. Milk or lemon?"

I blinked. "Milk, please."

The boy scooted off, and I turned to the sheriff. "Milk? In the air? They can do that?"

Sheriff Whitmore grinned. "Of course. I'm sure when he gets back, we can talk him into a tour of the facilities."

"What? Uh..." I was surprised by his reply and shook my head to clear it. "Why?"

"Because we're in the VIP suite, your brother instructed them to give you whatever we need, and it's what I'd do."

That dangerous glint in his eye stole my breath. I turned away. "Is there a bathroom? Somewhere I could freshen up?"

"Straight ahead. Push the panelling and the door will open." His voice contained amusement, and I marched off without answering because I didn't quite know how to cope. The door swung wide, and I entered a large and well-appointed bathroom. The tiles gleaming, a blinding white contrasted against dark wood.

I set about my business, then used the brush on the side and tidied my hair. Funny, before living with my brother, it wouldn't have bothered me, but now...

Or is it the sheriff? a sly whisper in my brain asked.

"Stop it."

Gazing into the mirror, I saw myself. Pleasant enough to look at. Nothing about me had changed, and yet...

These waters could swamp you, my psyche added.

I sighed, turned away from the looking glass, and re-entered the salon. The sheriff waited, his back to me, and I took a moment to study him. Tall and muscular with long dark hair. An imposing figure.

Something about his air spoke of danger and primitive emotions barely held in check. Though when he'd talked about Letitia's children, a softness overlaid that harsh quality he exuded.

What will he be like when he has his own children? The thought drew me up. I didn't know if he had any now. He could be married for all I knew.

My gaze snaked to his hand. No telltale ring such as Andrew wore. For a moment, something long buried uncurled itself within my chest.

Interest. Interest in the man who stood before me.

I bit my lip. He wasn't for me, and I wasn't for him. *Stop weaving fantasies!*

Settling myself back on the chaise, I stilled the sudden urge to move around in the vain hope that I could wash off these unfamiliar emotions that were all too difficult to accept.

Control. It will help you cope, I told myself. *Just like you've been trained your whole life.*

Clearly the sheriff heard me slide onto the seat, because he turned back and settled himself opposite me in one of the wing chairs.

The burn of his gaze unnerved me.

The urge to speak rose, and I let it take me. "Why were you sent to Haven?"

For a moment, silence stretched between us. "I was born near there. My father died when I was young, in an accident while testing early automatons. He'd been collaborating with your brother on the building of security equipment. There was a failure at the plant, and my father was crushed. Mr Coultihan—your father—cared for my mother and me."

A knot of regret took up residence in my belly. "I'm sorry to hear that." So little, and yet, what else was there to say? I knew loss. Had experienced it as a child.

The sheriff shrugged. "My mother put up with a lot during the marriage. He wasn't a great husband or role model. She said his death freed her to do things a married woman couldn't. She'd been raised in a progressive household. After Father's death, we went back there. Home."

His words hypnotized me. Freedom and progressive. Two words I knew but barely understood.

"Progressive?" I prompted.

"She wanted to study. Become a physiotraducere."

Now I blinked. It wasn't a term I'd heard before. "A what?"

He grinned, and my breath caught somewhere near my diaphragm.

"A medical doctor who specialises in transplantation of cybernetic parts to replace the missing, amputated, or unhealthy parts. Eyes, limbs, and so on."

Like Junior.

I shivered. "Where does she—" I swallowed deep, absorbing the frisson of fear. "—practice?"

"She died. Two years ago. Someone broke in while she was operating on a child who'd fallen in front of a tram. It's thought that they were someone who believed such practices should be reserved only for the exclusive upper echelons, because there were threats delivered to the clinic in the weeks prior to the attack. We believe the attacker was 'enhanced'." His voice took on a deep and coldly menacing tone. "We could tell because they left a calling card. They smashed through the table, and a tiny cog wheel was found caught in the debris."

I looked away, horrified by what he was telling me. "The child?"

"Died too."

When I glanced back, there was a tiny sheen of pain in his eyes, tell-tale moisture, but I didn't speak or move. Here stood a brave, proud man, and I wouldn't injure him with my clumsy attempts at comfort. My gut lurched uncertainly at the bare descriptions he'd drawn for me.

"It's not right," I whispered as I stood and moved to the window. Spread out below me was a patchwork of fields and trees. They seemed so small, almost insignificant, yet they lived, fought, and died for the land, those people below. They weren't insignificant, and neither was I, nor the sheriff's mother. "How do you cope with all this hate and horror?"

His hand clasped my shoulder. I hadn't heard the large man moving silently, yet he offered support without a word.

"I work hard. I protect those who deserve it, and I always remember what it's like to be lost and alone."

The last bit tore into me. A jagged knife that bit into my soul.

Closing my eyes, I inhaled deeply, trying to calm the emotions that swirled and threatened to drown me. "I... A cup of tea." I could hear the desperation in my voice, but I had to regain control.

"I'll pull the bell, see where the tea has gotten to."

I grabbed the rail that framed the window and held on until the boiling sensation passed, because staying upright and hanging on to my precious control pressed in on me.

Long seconds passed where I breathed in and out, concentrating on the way my lungs filled until I was once more steady and able to face everything I knew, had heard, and experienced.

I turned now, the swish of the gown I'd worn the only sound. My gaze found the sheriff's. He'd lowered himself into the chair and watched me.

"So, tell me, Sheriff. What happens when we reach the governor?"

He blinked. "We aren't actually going to the governor's today."

"Pardon?"

"I mean, we're going to see him eventually. Just not yet. You're going into a kind of protective custody, if you will." His face took on the bland mask of someone prevaricating well.

"Why?"

He harrumphed. "We should discuss this later." Now he rubbed his brow as if it ached.

"Why not now?" I stepped closer while his eyes tracked my moves, following every step.

"When we get where we're going."

"And that is?" I kept pushing, and he smiled, a long lazy grin that stole my breath all over again.

"Somewhere safe."

I pushed again, and he shook his head.

Just as I was ready to demand, a knock came at the door. I rushed over and pulled it open to find the young cabin boy on the other side with a tea tray in his hands.

The time for discussion had come and gone. Patience was once more the key.

The dirigible landed at a large wharf with tethers rising high into the air. I stepped through the opening and onto the gangway. Voices echoed and shouted while the vision of the town in the distance filled my view. Buildings, squat and grimy, sat opposite the wharf. Dark and menacing laneways interspersed them.

The road between the wharf and buildings was lightly cobbled, and carts, carriages, and horses filled it.

People milled and hurried about, and the whole time, my anchor was the sheriff beside me. He held me protectively close, yet never exceeded the bounds of appropriateness.

How do I feel about that? I didn't have an answer.

With a quick move, I dragged my wrap closer around my body and peered through the gathering gloom.

A large carriage rolled into view, a crest adorning the door: The Coultihan Dirigible Company.

"It appears your brother arranged transport for us." There was a hint of surprise in the sheriff's tone.

"So, we should be quick?" Yet even as I moved to make my way down the gangplank, his large hand stayed my moves.

"Not yet. Let's just watch for a moment, shall we?"

"But—"

"Shhhh."

We stood there as the people alighting swarmed past us. I glanced up, noting the intensity of his stare.

"You think..."

"It's all a little too convenient," he replied and then tugged me back within the confines of the covered walkway. "We might just find our own transport, and I'll send a message."

A trace of fear skittered along my nerves. *He senses something wrong.* Even though it would be simple to pull away and head down that ramp, my instincts warned me to trust the sheriff. My brother had obviously believed in him enough to send me with him, after all.

He grabbed my hand. I squeaked, "What—"

"Shhh, follow my lead. Answer only when I indicate."

Unused to prevarication, I wondered if I could, but he was already pulling me along toward the second-class line. "Slide your wrap over your head." He tugged at his badge, removing it and sliding it into a pocket as I watched.

I complied, and he dragged me into the line of families with young children.

"Look down and trust me."

We joined the crush, stepping carefully down the jouncing plank until our feet hit the dirt.

"Hold tight now," he whispered.

My hand was joined with his, either a death grip or lifeline. I couldn't be sure which was more accurate.

People jostled, children called and raced, and babies wailed. At the bottom of the steps, he tugged his hat farther down on his head and dragged me to the side. A stack of crates sat there, and we inched in behind them, the fence at our back. Clearly he didn't intend to be seen. I watched the way he looked, left, right, then left again. Every move drove a spike of warning into my chest.

"You're worried," I whispered, and he grunted while pulling me closer. "Sher—"

"Shh." He waited, gaze firmly on the carriage. "We need to wait until the carriage leaves and note if anyone follows it." He kept his voice low.

A finger of cold wiggled within my belly. Did he believe someone was on the lookout for us? Were we in danger? Surely not!

It felt like hours passed. My heart raced while the sounds slowly quieted, and the crowd melted away.

The driver got down from the top of the carriage, then moved over to the now-empty first-class gangway and conferred with the steward waiting there. The steward gave a shrug and headed up the plank while the driver waited. Time passed. The steward returned, and they spoke animatedly; then they traipsed back to the carriage, looking here and there.

Sheriff Whitmore released my fingers, and I exhaled. The driver clambered up to his post once more, and the vehicle rolled forward.

From a corner of the building opposite, a man emerged, his horse moving slowly as they followed the carriage.

The sheriff waited a little longer before dragging me out. "We need to hurry." He hailed the last cab waiting, a dusty, grimy contraption with a nag at the front.

"Wait here while I get our bags. Then we'll be back," he told the man, and the driver tipped his flattened cap.

I followed the sheriff to the gangway we were meant to use, and he conferred with one of the dirigible company's stewards. Our bags were carried over. "You've missed your personal carriage, sir. It came and went without you."

The sheriff didn't answer, just collected the three soft bags and hefted them into an anonymous rented carriage. "Should anyone make enquiries, you don't know where we went."

The steward gaped at him, then nodded in two sharp jerks.

I was handed into the cab, its interior as dusty and murky as I'd expected. Then he joined me inside.

"Drive to the nearest hotel. Then I'll give you instructions," he said to the driver. I didn't catch the reply, just a mumble.

The sheriff had mounded the bags on the seat opposite and settled beside me. In the sudden gloom, I could catch a whiff of his scent. Leather and man. Beneath all that, there was a hint of spice, rather like cinnamon.

To clear my mind, I inhaled deeply, and the scent of him grew, filling my mind so I could barely think straight, it was so overwhelming. Meanwhile, in my chest, something moved, jolting me into an awareness I wasn't sure I was ready to deal with.

The carriage pulled up outside a hovel, the front door slapping in the breeze as curtains waved. Clearly, this was aimed at those with little coin, sitting on the outskirts of town.

The sheriff climbed out, headed to the front of the carriage, and conferred with the driver. I waited inside as he completed his task, breathing easier once he entered the carriage again. It rolled forward.

"We'll be there soon. I've given instructions for us to travel to an alternative location, where we'll stay tonight. In the morning we'll move to the safe house."

"Why? Why can't we go straight there?" I bit my lip, more than aware that the question might sound inane.

The man beside me leaned in, his mouth near my ear, and I shivered at the intimacy of the actions. "There're several factors. The first is we'll access our own conveyance in the morning, and the other is we don't want to tip off where we're staying. I'm not sure just how close-mouthed this driver is."

"Do you think someone will really go to those kinds of lengths to find out where we are?"

"Yes I do, Ammy."

The answer startled me. Not because of the answer, but the way he said my name, like it was molten honey with a trace of some deeper emotion I refused to examine.

I glanced at him, noting the glint in his eye. "We'll talk when we reach our hotel."

I nodded and turned back, because I couldn't think of any other action that didn't betray my sudden nerves.

The hotel was one of those places that could be anywhere. It was almost a boarding house. The rooms were comfortably appointed, but it was literally just a room, with a smallish bed, a chest of drawers, and a mirror.

The sheriff turned to me and grimaced. "It's the best we can do for tonight."

I bit my lip.

Downstairs, when we'd taken the room for the night, he'd only asked for a single room. I'd opened my mouth, about to mention we required two, but he stayed with me, one hand gripping my wrist. That and the tiny shake of his head had the words dying on my lips.

"So, why just this room? Why not two?" I whirled now to face him.

"They'll be looking for a man and a woman travelling together but unmarried. Given the belief system, they won't be looking for a couple sharing a room. It also means we don't raise suspicions and have a room denied." The look on his face told me clearly that he also wasn't overly happy about the arrangement.

I blinked. It made sense. Sort of.

"But where will you sleep?"

He sighed. "With you."

"But..."

The sheriff shook his head even as my nerves quivered and jumped in response.

"We'll have to share the bed. There's not enough room on the floor and no seat."

"But I've... I can't..." The words didn't come out. I wanted to say I'd never considered spending the night in a bed with a man. The thought was scandalous. At worst, it might just test me beyond the boundaries I had imposed on myself.

Being next to the sheriff all night, his body nestled against mine—and it would be, as the bed was narrow—was wrong. Tempting.

My body flooded with heat.

He tugged off his hat and laid it down on the chest of drawers. "It's what we've got. We'll have to make the best of it."

My eyes strayed to the spotted mirror. His gaze met mine, and it was like all the air was sucked from my lungs. The telltale red flood on my face flared hotter.

"It's not seemly." The words emerged half strangled from me.

"I'll try to keep my hands to myself." He grinned now, and I squeaked. His hand landed on my shoulder. "We should go down, order a meal, then retire early. Tomorrow's going to be a little more difficult."

Frowning, I wondered how that could be. I'd been drugged, sent off on a dirigible, landed in a city I didn't know with a man I was neither related to nor married to. We'd hidden from someone watching us, taken a dirty cab, and landed in a hotel with one bed.

"I'm not sure that's possible," I muttered.

The sheriff remained silent, simply pouring water into the bowl and washing up. When he was done, he waited while I straightened my hair, then rifled through the large bag, found a shawl to replace my jacket, and shook out my skirts a final time.

"I'm ready," I stated.

He stood by the door, his eyes hooded as he watched.

"Not quite." He reached into the pocket of his waistcoat and retrieved something, then held it out to me. "You should put this on."

"What is it?"

He grimaced. "A wedding ring."

Shock coursed through me. "A wedding ring?"

His slow nod and the intensity of his gaze stole my breath. "In case anyone asks questions. Gives the situation some believability."

His words made sense, but still I couldn't seem to move. I didn't know why such a simple thing—and ruse—discombobulated me.

With a sigh, he plucked it from my grip, drew off my left glove, and held my hand in a firm grasp. "Ammy?"

I may have looked up at him, but I was busy trying to hold in my reaction to the slide of that gold band onto my finger. It didn't matter that my brain knew it was a lie. It didn't matter that we weren't really married, because all I could focus on was the gravity of the action he was performing.

Hot tears pricked my eyes, and I blinked.

"Ammy?"

I looked up through the veil of moisture.

His Adam's apple bobbed, and his hand shook. "Ammy?"

"No." I stepped back, breaking the invisible connection between us. "We should go." I waited a moment until he turned, hand reaching for the door. Without his searching gaze on me, I could breathe again. I did, and a deep and unsteady sound betrayed my confusion.

Did he hear it? If so, he didn't react, just stepped out of the way so I could pass him.

Chapter Five

Dinner was a basic affair. Meat, vegetables, and a thick, glutinous gravy. The cooking was about as you'd expect in a hole-in-the-wall hotel, but it was filling. Maybe not as good as I'd gotten used to in my brother's house, but I had a full belly at the end.

"So, what happens next?" The query was carefully formed by me, and the sheriff stared at my face.

"We head up to the room and bed."

If I hadn't been prepared, I may have been surprised by his comment.

"I mean working out who's following us. Or attempting to."

He placed his utensils on the plate, then dabbed carefully at his mouth. I had the impression he was drawing time out. Why? It seemed patience was the only way to find out.

"We discuss this tomorrow. However, *wife*," he emphasized, "it's time to retire."

My face flamed as the heat scorched through me.

Rising, I kept my gaze focused on the stairs and headed in that direction. At the bottom of the steps, the sheriff stopped me. Looking at him, I noticed the narrowing of his eyes, the way his face tightened.

"I'll go first," he said, and I moved aside to follow him.

They creaked with every step, and once we gained the upper landing, he stopped me. "Wait here."

He moved to the door, fishing the key out and turning it. No sound, not even a squeak. The door swung wide, and he entered.

Silence.

My heart thudded with this overwhelming rhythm that indicated he expected the worst, while an icy trickle of sweat slid down my back under the confines of my heavy gown and underwear.

When he came back, his face was grim.

"She—"

He laid a quiet hand against my mouth. "We should retire." There was a dangerous note that only someone who knew him would understand. He curled his hand around mine and tugged me into the room.

"What was that all about?" My voice wobbled slightly, but I would not be cowed. For the first time in living memory, I refused to accept some ridiculous story, but he simply shook his head.

I removed my shawl and considered changing into the nightgown Gloriana had stashed for me, but that indicated an intimacy I had no interest in sharing. Instead, I looked at my skirt and sighed, removing it. Sleeping in my petticoats wasn't something I'd planned on, but at least with so many layers I'd feel some modicum of control.

The sheriff had turned his back while I'd shuffled through the bag, and now he dragged the single heavy armchair before the door and settled in it. I jumped at the scraping noise and scurried to the bed, the whole time mightily aware of his presence.

I tugged at the bed covers and slid under them.

"You should at least change out of your corset."

His dry words made every nerve in my body quiver, but the corset represented a lot more than just a piece of clothing. It was like a shield, protecting me from urges I was trying so hard to ignore.

"Uh, no, thank you. I'm fine." Lying there in the gas-lit room, with the whalebone digging into the soft flesh of my back, I knew it would be a long and painful night.

"If you insist." He shoved away from the chair and came to stand over the bed, glaring down at me. With slow movements, the sheriff reached for his jacket and shrugged it off.

"What—" An enormous ball of something filled my throat as I blinked several times in quick succession. "What are you doing?"

"Getting ready for bed," he informed me, and that ball swelled in size to a mountain.

"In here?" I squeaked.

"There's nowhere else to sleep, and that's what we both need." Waistcoat now divested as well, he sat on the side of the bed. It dipped under his weight and squeaked while he removed one boot, then the other.

With a quick move, he levered up so he now lay beside me, then dimmed the light. "Goodnight, Ammy."

I squeezed my eyes closed, trying to shut out the sight of him and the awareness that he lay beside me, albeit on top of the covers.

Time passed slowly, as I heard the *tick-tock* of the clock on top of the chest of drawers.

I heard the evenness of his breathing, felt the heat radiating from his body, and that awareness had parts of me reacting in ways I was unprepared for and really didn't want. There was a warmth spreading through my belly and loins while my chest tingled.

I wanted things I had no right to want.

Like his arms around me.

His lips on mine.

"I won't touch you unless you want it, Ammy."

His words startled me. They were dark and hazy with passion, and I wanted more than anything to give in to the drugging and mesmerising tones. I wanted all of him and so much more. I clenched my hands tight, hoping to ward off that secret longing that filled me up and hollowed me out.

"I..." What was there to say? "Goodnight." I took the coward's exit, but tears stung my eyes.

He shifted onto his side, away from me, but I lay still, staring at the ceiling, ignoring my clamouring body. Nothing had ever seemed as hard as this.

Morning came swiftly, the sun fitful and watery, shining through the glass, only broken by the grey lace at the window.

I rose swiftly and set about climbing into my skirt. I reached for the buttons to find my fingers brushed away.

"Let me assist." His breath whispered over the sensitive skin of my nape.

Much as I wanted to say I could do it myself, his fingers were already there.

Is he torturing me? I swallowed hard.

He'd already dressed, and we shoved everything back into the small valises we'd brought with us.

"Today will be long. Stay close. If we get separated, find a bakery and wait for me."

Shock and surprise cascaded through me, and I stared at him. If I were him, I'd probably want to laugh, but his face didn't change. "A bakery?"

He smiled, and it twisted the knife in my guts, because some tiny seed of hope was blooming. "No one ever thinks to look there." As he spoke, he shoved a wad of money into my pocket. "Just in case. There's an address there too, but only if there's no other way." He cleared his throat. "But I will come for you, Ammy."

Our eyes met as if he were trying to impart some dark truth to me. I nodded, and the tension that had filled him seeped away a bit.

He took my hand, and even with the layers of gloves, I still felt his heat. We headed downstairs and out the door.

The streets were deserted except for the few moving about their business in the early morning hours. He looped my arm through his, and we walked. I knew what he was doing. For all the world, we looked like a couple, fresh in from the country, looking for somewhere to begin a life together.

Our gait was unhurried as we traipsed up one street, crossed a thoroughfare, and headed down a lane. Through a gate and out to the other side of a backyard and onto another street.

After what felt like hours, he hailed a cab, and we pushed inside. He gave directions, and we moved at a more rapid pace before ending outside a theatre.

"How long—"

"Shhh," he answered, waiting as the cab we'd just climbed out of headed off. He pulled me into a doorway. "We've been seen."

"Really? I fail—"

He ended my words with his lips against mine. They were warm, firm, and mobile against my own. I dropped my bag and reached up, holding on to his shoulder.

Long seconds passed as my fingers held tight, seeking purchase. Then he pulled away.

"This is the dangerous part. Stay close," he murmured, and our gazes collided.

A sound, loud and booming, had me half turning.

The sheriff grabbed my shoulder and drove me to the ground as bits of wood flittered down around us.

"They've found us. Quick, crawl around the side, then head down the lane. Don't stop. Don't look back." He spoke urgently, and something inside me lurched.

The danger is real.

He shoved me, and I finally moved, following his instructions. My feet slipped as I made to rise, then found purchase on the damp soil, still clinging tightly to the small bag I'd been carrying. I followed the path between the buildings, got to the other end, and ducked into the nearest shop.

A bakery.

"No..." I laughed, high-pitched and on edge as I settled into a seat in a darker corner. The building was nearly empty, and a woman sauntered over. I gulped and blinked. I'd need to order something, or she'd think something was wrong.

"Tea?" The woman stared at me for several long seconds.

I nodded furiously, shoving my bag beneath the table and finding the small stash of notes he'd shoved into my pocket just this morning. "Yes. Bring two cups. A friend may join me." It took every ounce of self-possession to settle myself, but at least I sounded normal enough, if a little winded.

The woman retreated, and I laid my hands in my lap. They twisted the heavy material of my skirt, but outwardly I would project a calm facade.

The tea came, and I drank slowly, waiting the whole time for someone to arrive. Someone looking for me. Every time the door opened, I started.

Eventually, I finished the drink and wondered what to do with myself. *Where should I go?*

The door opened again, the bell pealing. I looked up, and there he was. The sheriff. I couldn't control the sudden quiver of my lip or the dancing butterflies deep in my stomach.

Emotions I'd tamped down hard crashed around me. I dropped my head so he wouldn't read them on my face. I didn't want to even acknowledge them, but they remained there.

He advanced, stood looking down at me, the heat of his gaze searing. The chair scraped back on the wood floors before he sat opposite me. "You aren't injured?" His words raked over my mind like fingers on a chalkboard.

I shook my head, unsure that I'd be able to answer without giving everything away.

He reached out, took my hand in his, and I turned to gaze upon him.

I felt the frisson of connection between us. "I thought you'd been hurt. Captured." I licked my lips, and when our eyes met, his were dark with intense emotion.

"No. But we should leave."

I nodded and rose, as did he, the heat of his resting hand low on the curve of my back. Even through the layers of cloth, it scorched me.

A dark carriage, horseless and with a driver waiting, sat near the shopfront. The sheriff urged me forward and in. "The residence," he commanded.

Once the door shut behind us, bags dropped to the floor, he pulled me forward. "I'm glad I found you safe. They know we're here."

Fury bubbled to the surface. "Who? Who knows we're here, and how? Why?"

In the gloom, his eyes glinted. "I'll tell all when we arrive. Soon."

It wasn't enough to calm the waves that crashed inside me, but I held on to my emotions because I'd learned early not to question. Not to push for more information than a man would freely give. I'd learned never to show my emotions.

A new side of me was emerging, though, and she—this new Amaryllis—wouldn't be contained for long. The thought scared me while it also freed me from the constraints I'd endured in the years I'd been held by them.

We turned a corner, and the carriage sped up. "Where...?"

His fingers curled around mine. "We won't take long."

I wanted to curl in now, to bask in the sense of well-being that came with his words and the fantasies I'd been unable to escape since I'd first seen him.

It took every ounce of willpower to pull away, but I did. Now I glanced through the glass, watching as we entered the heart of the city, past buildings that towered into the heavens. Some appeared six and seven stories high. "They're so big!"

He grinned. "Not really. I hear New Jerome has higher buildings again."

I turned. "You've been there?"

He shook his head. "No. But Gloriana and Andrew have."

I sat back and considered his words. "You've known them for a long time?"

"Something like that. I told you about my mother and father. Andrew kept in touch, and when the chance came to swing back around your way, well, I wanted to do my part."

"You chose this assignment?"

"Sort of." He narrowed his gaze and shrank back against the seat. "Sit back and be quiet."

His hand dug down at the holster on his hip, and I sucked in a deep breath, following his instructions.

A tiny unit, a ball with cogs and a large monocle-type eye, whirred past the carriage.

I opened my mouth, but he shook his head. He did, however, tug at my shawl, and awareness spread through me. I pulled it over my head as he slouched in his seat and dipped his chin, though I could see the tension surrounding him, the way his gaze kept track of the window.

With handkerchief in hand, I mock-dabbed at my eyes and waited. The tiny machine came back, hovered for a moment outside, and whirred before flying off.

"Was that...?" I couldn't finish because my mind was overcome with the reality. Someone was looking for us.

"Yes. Once we reach the Retreat, we'll be safe."

The carriage moved slowly, far too slowly to soothe the rapid cadence of my heart, as we moved farther into the city.

Finally, a large black gate of iron slid open, and we rolled within.

The portico, solid marble by its appearance, loomed over us, as the carriage stopped at a set of stairs. "Welcome back, sir."

He handed me down and inside, letting a breath whoosh out once the heavy wood doors clanged shut behind us.

"Come this way." He started down the hall, and for the first time, I wondered where we were. He was clearly at ease here in this gigantic house. It was furnished in dark wood, with pastoral images surrounded in gilt all over the walls.

I glanced down. My footfalls were silenced by a long runner, the wine-red and verdant green thick beneath my feet.

Looking up, I noted the way he watched me. "What is this place?"

His smile widened. "My home."

In the bedchamber I'd been assigned, I blinked as I worked on coming to terms with what I'd just learned.

This was the sheriff's home.

A large mansion in the middle of the city.

The imposing four-storey home was well appointed with immense windows peering out onto what I could only describe as a private park. The house itself boasted a landing full of bedrooms, with solid, heavy, but impeccable furnishings. Not one speck of dust in sight, and staff enough to serve a palace.

A young lady who'd introduced herself as Jessie had already come in and was even now bustling around the room. It seemed she'd ordered a bath to be drawn in the bathing room, and I watched her giving orders from the deeply cushioned lounge. It was downright surreal. First moving from Haven House to Andrew and Gloriana's estate, and now to this.

"Uh, Jessie?"

The girl turned in my direction. "Yes, Miss Amaryllis?"

"Tell me about the sheriff."

Her smile faded a little. "He doesn't come here much anymore, miss. Not since his mother passed, God rest her soul."

Not quite the answer I expected. So I waited, hoping she'd shed more light on the situation. She resumed the unpacking and hanging of the few items of clothing inside the bag.

Another maid scurried into the room. "The bath is ready." Then the girl bobbed a quick curtsy and left the bedroom.

Jessie gestured me into the bathing room, then shut the door and set about assisting me with undressing. Once again, the sense of being in a world I didn't know and couldn't understand filled my head.

I slid into the deep bath with a sigh of relief. Jessie hiked up a sleeve, and I saw the implant. "Your arm," I gasped.

Jessie turned and smiled. "The sheriff's mother fixed me. I was in a nasty accident not long after she began her practice. All the other doctors wanted to cut it off, but she looked and said she'd make it right again." She flexed the muscles, and for the first time, I heard the whirr of moving parts.

"How did...?"

The smile Jessie turned toward me was filled with gratitude. "She knew I'd never get normal work with my injuries and the cynetic implants, are reserved for the rich, or those who do bad things. So she hired me. Had me trained as her personal maid, and I'll be eternally grateful for that. When she died, the sheriff kept me on. Told me one day he'd need my help." The sigh she released was full of sadness. "But he's never here. Too busy working for the law and his special team dealing with those religious fools."

I bit my lip. "Religious fools" certainly described the situation I'd found myself in. After all, couldn't the Haven situation be characterised as a cult? It didn't explain how he went from poor at the time of his father's death to this mansion, though.

The need to find out rose in my throat, but I squashed it down. I refused to pry. It was his business, yet it didn't exactly make sense, and if I couldn't understand it, my discomfort levels always rose expeditiously.

I considered Jessie's explanation. Many questions ran through my head, but I wanted to know more about the terminology raised. "So, you call them cynetic implants. Aren't they cyborg-kinetic?" I frowned and bit my lip, wondering if that could be considered prying.

Jessie blinked, then returned a sunny smile. "Oh, well, Dr Whitmore was different in her approach to dealing with infirmities like mine. Most people have whole implants or replacements, such as arms, legs, and hands. She trialled something entirely different. She knew many of us would have to face ridicule and might be treated badly, so she considered that by performing a partial removal and replacement, it would be less visible. I was one of the first she tried this new therapy on. They replace what's under the skin but use a true skin to overlay it, so it's out of sight."

I shook my head and picked up the washcloth, applying it to my body as I considered her words.

Certainly, in my experience, I'd seen many who were treated poorly with implantation and replacement therapies, but when I thought of Junior, fear was the first and most major concern that came to mind. He was a horrible man. A bully. His replacement had been merely to give the appearance of strength and the power that came with money. For him, it was all about the status.

"How could you afford it?"

She tittered. "The doctor was a kind lady. After hours, she'd take on those of us who couldn't afford to pay. We would then offer something in return, be it working in the clinic or something similar. Nothing onerous, but it's how she allowed us to repay her act of kindness. My mother was a dressmaker, so she made gowns for the doctor, things like that."

I rolled the information over in my thoughts as I finished bathing. When I was ready, I stood, and Jessie handed me the towel. I took it, lost in my thoughts, and followed her back into the bedroom.

Clothes I'd never seen waited for me, and I turned. "Whose are these?"

Jessie smiled. "They were sent here yesterday for you. I believe from Mrs Coultihan."

"They knew," I murmured. It seemed I was the last to know, as always.

Dinner was quiet, with the sheriff lost in thought and me wondering how I'd possibly amuse myself for the next however long I'd be here.

"Prisoner" wasn't quite the word I could use to describe the situation I now found myself in, but whatever word fit more appropriately, well, I couldn't really say.

Certainly the house was comfortable. It had already been made clear to me that whatever I needed or requested, within reasonable boundaries, would be made available. Yet I was at a loose end, unable to wander or leave the house.

That led to my next conundrum. While the remains of the meal were taken away, I cleared my throat. "Could I perhaps look in the library? See if there's reading material I might borrow?"

The sheriff looked at me. "Of course. You have only to ask." His smile was absent, as if he were working through some odd issue that only now came to mind.

"I should retire for the evening, then," I muttered and rose.

"Ammy?"

His voice stilled me as I turned away. I didn't turn back because I wasn't really sure what he'd say, and whether it wouldn't be more than I can deal with.

"You don't have to leave. I know I haven't been the best of company tonight, but I enjoy having you near."

Oh Lord! My mouth dried up, and I wanted to turn, to stay, but I wasn't ready to deal with any kind of connection between us. What came next? When would I be ready? Would I ever be prepared? Questions too big for me to answer right now. "I'm exhausted, Sheriff."

"Damien," he corrected me.

I shook my head, because his gentle reminder had my belly churning with emotions I didn't want to consider. "Sheriff," I said, reinforcing to both of us the need for that separation between us.

"Damien." I hadn't heard him move behind me, but suddenly he was there, his hands holding me in place.

Heat enveloped me, and the whisper of his breath caressed the back of my skin. God, I wanted to squirm, to turn and burrow myself into his embrace. I squeezed my eyes shut even as my body betrayed me, the finest shiver starting as nerve endings danced and jumped.

"Say it, Ammy."

"Da... Damien." It came out as a whisper, though my voice sounded unlike my own. Thick.

"Yes," he said.

Behind my closed lids, stars exploded. My breathing came in rapid pants.

"Ammy?"

He turned me, and I held my eyes closed even as my body demanded I should open them, look at him.

"Open your eyes."

They fluttered open, and there he was, his face harsher than I'd seen before. His eyes glinted in the lamplight.

"Damien?" I didn't know what I was asking, but the word slipped from my mouth, the question hanging between us.

I swayed toward him, and our lips met.

Touched.

Soft, like the wing of a butterfly, before he slid away again.

In that short while, I lost control of myself and my emotions as bones melted and needs swelled. A languor spread through me, one wholly alien and yet so exciting!

He smiled, a masculine symbol of satisfaction. "You should go to bed, Ammy."

I blinked. "I... What?"

He reached out, brushed a loose curl from my face. "Go to bed. Otherwise, I'm going to want more than you're prepared for." In his words lay a promise, dark and hungry.

I stepped back, noting the predator. "I... Yes, I'll visit the library in the morning."

His fingers dropped away, and I could breathe again without the intoxicating scent of Damien there to befuddle me.

"Goodnight," I muttered and fled, feet moving swiftly over the deep carpeting as I reached for the door. The urge to turn back, to see if he watched, filled me, and I ruthlessly tamped it down, swung through the door, and headed to my chamber.

No man will own me. No man will dictate my decisions.

If only I could believe that!

Chapter Six

Morning light shone through the windows, but I was already awake, dressed, and sitting at the small escritoire when Jessie joined me.

"Morning, miss." She bobbed a curtsy.

"Please don't," I begged.

Jessie goggled at me.

"My name is Amaryllis. Use it," I urged. "I'm no noble lady or gently born princess." I cleared my throat. "I take it breakfast is in the dining room?" When Jessie shook her head, I sighed. "Where, then?"

"The sheriff prefers to eat in the small parlour. I'll show you the way."

I rose and followed the girl down the stairs and through a maze of hallways. "If you need me, Miss Amaryllis, just press the bell." She scooted off.

I suppose I should be glad she didn't curtsy again and announce me into the room.

While my stomach tied itself in knots, I laid my hand on the doorknob. The metal was cold, but I sighed and entered. *Nothing ever gets better from waiting.*

A fire crackled in the hearth, scents of coffee and bacon wafted in the air, and my stomach gurgled in recognition. At least the room appeared to be empty, so embarrassment was the least of my concerns. I headed to the table, picked up a plate, and moved to the sideboard where warming dishes lay. I lifted the lid, inhaled the scent of pig meat, and scooped up an egg, tomato, and a succulent-looking sausage.

Settling into the chair, I picked up the knife and fork and ate, when the door opened again. In he strode. Damien. The sheriff and the man who had taken up most of my dreams.

"Good morning, Ammy. Did you sleep well?"

I wanted to snarl but contained it. He looked rested, comfortable, and at ease, whereas I'd spent the night tossing and turning, thinking about him and that kiss.

"Fine, thank you for asking," I lied through my teeth.

The glint in his eyes informed me that he knew I prevaricated.

"Wonderful day, isn't it?" He reached for a plate and began piling food on it.

With a determination I didn't know I had, I settled into my breakfast, though any sense of interest in it had waned. The textures and flavours I'd relished before he'd entered the room could have been sawdust now. After all, here was a much tastier morsel, if the memory of his lips against mine and the essence of him was correct.

In silence, I set down the utensils and reached for my coffee, draining the cup before carefully dabbing at my lips. Perhaps if I were quick, I could escape—

"Don't rush on my account, Ammy." I heard the humour lacing his voice.

"I'm done," I answered, rising from the chair.

"I'd like to talk to you." He indicated for me to sit with his hands.

Like any agreeable guest, I sank back down, cursing inwardly that I'd waited so long to break my fast. "Of course."

"You're uncomfortable now. I apologise. Last night was, while not inexcusable, perhaps an unwise action on my part."

I looked at my plate. If I looked at him, he'd read the sudden weakness that filled me. Weakness that he now regretted his actions while I'd obviously taken them to mean something significantly different.

I didn't want it. The biggest lie of all. If I were honest with myself, I felt maybe not complete but freed and excited by the action. The experience. None of which made any sense. My brain thrust into the ongoing debate inside me.

"I... Sheriff..." I fisted my hands, balled them so tight in my lap that I felt the blood rush when I released the pressure, then laid them palm down on my lap. "I appreciate that it was a mistake." Now I did glance at him, but only for a second because of the ferocity of his scowl.

"Don't mistake my words, Ammy. There was no *mistake* in my intent." His voice turned silky, and my insides melted just a little further. "I wanted to kiss you. I still do, but you aren't ready for what I crave."

The words sucked the oxygen from my lungs. "I..." Now I rose with jerking movements, and the chair fell. Fear congealed in the pit of my belly. "I have no interest in..." I waved my hands and stalked to the door, every move an act of bravado.

"Ammy." His voice stilled me.

Tears stung my eyes because, much as he might intrigue me, I couldn't give in. I'd seen what happened to women who gave up themselves for a man, and that wasn't the future I needed. Besides, soon, I'd be joined by children. They needed me more than I needed this man.

If only that were true.

"Please don't do this to me, Sheriff. I have a commitment."

"And I'll help you see it through, Ammy. But don't think that because you've given your word, you can't have more." I heard him advance, and that heated pit in my stomach shook, lapping at the walls I'd somehow built around myself. "And my name is Damien. Last night you used my name."

I clenched my hands tightly together. I wanted to turn to him. To say his name and watch the way his eyes shone with excitement.

"Say it again, Ammy. I need to hear my name on your lips."

"No," I whispered, because I wanted to call him Damien, and that filled me with a terrifying dread. A tear burst free and trickled down my cheek. I controlled the urge to dash it away, knowing that would tell him just how upset and affected I really was. That way led to danger, and I'd seen more than enough repercussions of weakness to last me a lifetime.

I wrenched toward the door, but he took my hand, spun me around. I closed my eyes and heard him draw in a deep and unsteady breath. "Tears, Ammy?" His hand swiped over my cheek. "Have I scared you?"

When I opened my eyes, it was to see deep pools of green, eternity in their depths. "No. I'm scaring myself." My voice wobbled like my knees.

His face crinkled. Damien didn't understand. How could he?

"I'm afraid of what I want. Of how you make me feel. I promised myself..." Now I gulped. This conversation had dived so deep in the blink of an eye, but I prided myself on my honesty. "I don't want the commitment and the work that comes with a husband. Children, yes, but not the *chains*." I spat the last word from my lips.

His face blanked. "Commitment and responsibility? Chains?"

I bit my lip, unsure how to proceed. Clearly I needed to explain better to make him see what I meant. "I lived a life of subservience. Where a man made every decision for the women in the household, immaterial of age, ability, or any other thing that might make them stand out. We were little more than chattels to be given and bought at whim. I don't want that for my future. I need to make my decisions for myself. To choose what I want. Who I want." My chest rose and fell under the onslaught of my sudden fury.

"I don't want to own you, Ammy." His quiet words wrapped themselves around me like a warm embrace, and my spine bent. I doubled over as the torrent of anguish escaped, a hot tide of horror, fear, and anger. I cried and shuddered as his arms enfolded me.

Damien held me close as I sobbed out the well of emotions I'd tried so hard to ignore for years; they broke and washed over us both. At some point he slid his arms under my legs and lifted me, the heat and security of him soothing the raggedness of my outburst. When I curled onto his lap, I burrowed in. His hands moved in a slow rub over my back. Comfort. Support.

Eventually I came back to me. I raised my head, though my brain was woolly and my eyes swollen. "I'm sorry," I croaked, swiping at the wetness coating my face.

"Never be sorry for sharing yourself with me. I don't suppose you've had many opportunities to do that before?" His grip on me didn't loosen, and to be honest, I didn't want it to.

I shook my head, hair sticking to the tacky moisture drying on my cheeks. I patted my pockets, searching for a handkerchief. "No... Oh dear." Embarrassment flooded me.

He moved, and a cloth of cotton quickly appeared in front of my gaze.

I wiped and blew, aware he waited for whatever I would do next.

Dropping the handkerchief to my lap, I wondered whether I should move or wait for him to let me go.

Two taps came on the door, and his chest vibrated as he gave the command to "Come."

I ducked my head down as the door opened, refusing to allow anyone else to see my weakness. "Sir, we have a communication from Haven. The children are on their way."

Children.

"She's..."

He nodded. "Yes. Andrew and Gloriana have been in contact with me. Letitia is failing, and they took custody yesterday, then arranged the airship. The children will arrive this evening."

The knot in my stomach that had melted away now reformed, heavier than before. "They'll need rooms, clothing." I pushed at Damien's arms. "I have to—"

"Already attended to." The rubbing started again at my back. "Thank you, Starson. I'll be along soon."

The door closed and left the two of us alone once more.

"I need to..." Squirming, I made to move away.

"Just a moment longer, Ammy." The entreaty warned me that the softness within him was buried deep and just as fragile as my own.

"But—"

"Take a moment to breathe. To stop."

So I did, letting the warmth of his body keep the frigidness that threatened to envelop me at bay for long moments.

"When you're ready, Ammy, I'll be here." I almost missed the words because he spoke so quietly.

"I'm afraid, Damien."

He shuddered beneath me. "You said my name." His voice took on a thick quality.

I had. In my mind, since this conversation began, somehow I'd changed my mind. Now he was no longer "the sheriff." He was Damien.

It felt important, this fact. Why or how, I wouldn't consider right now, because later today, I'd take on responsibility for children. Not mine, but they would be. I had promised their mother I'd ensure their safety. The promise went to the heart of who I saw myself to be. They wouldn't suffer for another day, because they were innocent, just as I'd once been.

He released me with a sigh. "You set the pace, Ammy. I won't push you. Never. One day, you'll wake and know I'm here, waiting for you."

How could he say these things? Mean them when he barely knew me?

When I was braver, stronger, I'd ask.

I slid away, rose, and smoothed my disordered skirts. "I need to make sure everything is right for them."

"Go. I'll still be here. Waiting."

The words strengthened me, and I left the room and him behind. But my mind knew that one day, I'd walk in there and ask for more.

Chapter Seven

The carriage pulled out of the driveway. Damien had been more than unwilling to allow me to join him, but I'd pleaded and argued until he'd finally agreed. The lines of his face were tight, and I knew he worried.

"Tell me the names of the children," I asked again, and he huffed out a sigh.

"Francesca is fourteen. She's taken over the mothering role to some extent, and Letitia fled to ensure she wasn't married off sooner rather than later."

I understood Letitia's fears all too well. However, I waited for Damien to continue.

"Then you have Simeon, aged seven, Samson, aged five, Constance is three, and Faith is two. They've all been damaged, Ammy."

"And you became involved because...?"

Damien grimaced. "Gloriana has powerful friends. When Letitia's illness became undeniable, Gloriana told me it wasn't the first instance of wasting illnesses she'd seen among these women. She feared for the children, since Letitia had suffered so much to save them from the life that loomed. The children were always her greatest concern, and she wanted to get them away from the clutches of her father."

I stared at out the front of the carriage. Five children under the age of fourteen were now my responsibility. I'd not really had much to do with Haven's children, as each mother cared for them. Would I be able to do the right thing? Make the right choices?

Damien reached out and took my hand. "You'll do fine, Ammy. You're gentle and kind but a fighter when you need to be."

Was he reading my mind? I shook my head, because now wasn't the time for introspection.

We swayed on the roads as we closed in on the area where we'd run to, hiding from those chasing us, and suddenly the wisdom of my argument dried up. What if they were waiting? Was my hard-headedness going to place the children in danger? I bit my lip as doubts assailed me.

The airship came into view, sailing over the tops of the trees and smaller buildings as it headed toward the dock. For a moment, I let the breathtaking beauty of it overtake me. It was magnificent. A thing of technological wonder, with the bulbous canopy and the lower ship-like structure.

Voices called, and ropes, long and sinuous despite their girth, slid down. They were grasped and tugged, and the movement of rudder and screw propeller became louder.

Without thinking, I gripped Damien's hand. "What a sight," I breathed.

"Indeed."

I turned to say something, but the words melted on my lips, now aware his gaze was focused on me. The intensity scorched my flesh, and in my breast, I felt the jump and quiver of anticipation.

A loud *whomp* broke the connection, and I realigned myself, staring at the airship and hoping I could ignore the pull between us.

The ship dropped slowly until it touched the ground. People scattered like ants before drops of rain; then the gangplanks slid up, the gates to the walking areas opened, and people appeared.

Soon, a flood of humanity exited from the ship, until at last a small band of staff escorted the children toward us. Damien rose and alighted from the carriage with an admonition to "Stay here." It irked, but I followed his advice. Bags were fastened to the back of the conveyance, and the children were ushered forward with speed.

They climbed in, Francesca taking the youngest up on her lap as the oldest boy did the same to the slightly older toddler.

Damien barely settled himself when a larger sound echoed.

Red filled my vision.

Flames seared.

"Go," he called to the driver. "Hold on to the children," he muttered and dug into the holster he'd fastened to his waist.

I dragged the youngest boy against me, then urged Francesca in beside me.

The carriage shot forward with a jerk, and we rattled and careened forward.

At a corner, we swayed precariously, the younger two crying.

Had they picked up my concern and fears? We moved swiftly, buildings blurring at the speed with which we hurtled through the streets.

Terror shot through me. *Are we out of control? Will we make it back to the house?*

Gradually the vehicle slowed, then came to a stop, and Damien climbed out. Tense moments passed before he clambered back in, his face a tense mask. "We need to get home. Then I'll contact your brother."

I opened my mouth to ask what he'd seen, but the way he looked at the children, then back to me, spoke volumes.

I gave in, and we rode in near silence, only the hiccupping sobs of the two little girls invading the quiet.

Once we were upon the house, the gates opened to admit us, and the tension that surrounded Damien seeped away—not totally, but enough that he could smile at the youngsters. We climbed down and headed into the house, Francesca, Simeon, and Samson looking up at the spacious ceiling.

"Francesca? Children? If you will go with Mrs Coltraine, the housekeeper, she'll see you to your rooms. Staff are also ready with some refreshments."

The words were soft and carefully modulated to likely ameliorate some hysterics from the present concerns.

As I made to escort them up the stairs, Damien's arm shot out. "When they're settled, come join me in my office. We'll talk there."

Whatever he had to say, I knew I wouldn't like it just from the lines of strain on his face. "Of course," I answered, and, taking the youngest girl in my arms, we made our way up the stairs.

Time passed, settling the children, then dealing with issues that arose. The dinner hour came and went. Night descended on the house, but Damien was curiously absent from the dinner table.

I wouldn't intrude. Clearly he was busy and hadn't sent for me, so I retired for the evening.

At midnight or thereabouts, I heard steps by my door. My heart thudded, wondering if he'd enter. Come talk with me about where he'd been and what he'd learned. But then they resumed, heading to the chamber down the hall, and I'd lain there, my heart thudding wildly.

Every noise of the house seemed to wake me, so I felt exhausted and wrung out by the time I woke.

Breakfast with the children had proved a laborious affair.

The youngest argued and tussled, whined and cried. The staff who'd been assigned to their care raced around, and I'd found myself at a loss until Francesca explained they were grieving in their own way.

"But your mother..." How did one explain that she'd sent them away before she'd succumbed to her illness?

Francesca grimaced. "I know what you're thinking. I know why she sent us here, and Simeon has an inkling. The others don't understand. They're too young." She'd spoken like a tiny, undergrown adult, and it shocked me to realise she was probably far worldlier than I was, having assist with both the birth of the children, and having seen the begetting too.

I'd stayed to assist until they were finally settled with amusements. Then I left the room, worn out and restless.

With the children in their suite at the centre of the house, I had a moment to stop, refresh myself, before heading down to talk with Damien. Whatever he'd seen, he'd known it would upset the children, so he'd kept it to himself, but time was now long past to find out what I didn't know.

We'd been attacked more than once, and the fact was, whatever brought this on was well beyond my ability to comprehend.

I swept into my bedchamber, thankful for the solitude. It wouldn't last, but for now, I let my gaze wander to the windows. What I saw in the distance stole my breath. The glow on the horizon was bad enough, but my view beyond the gardens showed a sight that terrified me more. Beyond the large metal fencing stood men. A veritable army. They were faced off by those within the garden, armed and no doubt ready to defend. They hadn't been there before.

Without considering, I stepped up to the window, gripping the wooden sill with nerveless fingers. "What's going on?" I murmured.

"They want the children, miss. They also want you." Jessie had entered the room while I'd been lost in my thoughts.

Now I whirled, facing her. "Why? Who wants us?"

She shrugged. "No one knows, or at least whatever they know, they're keeping to themselves. The sheriff has men throughout the house should they break through the perimeter. He's sending all the non-essential staff home."

I blinked. "What?"

"I'm to stay to assist with the children and yourself and the nanny, of course. He—the sheriff—wants me to pack some clothes, simple just in case we need to evacuate."

"Evacuate?" I felt dull. Wooden and totally lost. *Why? Why would we need to run again? We've already done that twice.*

Something inside me exploded, and fury washed through every part of my body. I'd just found somewhere I could breathe and was trying to sort through the mess of my mind. Now that was all being jeopardised again. "I don't even know why!" I jerked away, my body reacting to my wild confusion.

"Miss?" Jessie enquired, her face drawn, gaze keen.

Shaking my head, I fought my way back to the here and now. "Nothing, Jessie. Grab some clothes for me, then, as you've been instructed. We can arrange items for the children later. Meanwhile, the sheriff and I are going to have a conversation."

I left the room, my feet tapping on the floor as I headed for the stairs, then down. I stopped only long enough to fill my lungs with oxygen before rapping on his office door.

His imperious "Come" didn't settle me. I marched in, prepared to battle for the truth. I stopped short at the sight of Andrew, his face streaked and grey.

"An... Andrew?" I hurried forward, and he took my outstretched hands. "What's happened?"

He shook his head and took the seat Damien steered him to. "I had to come. We lost men on the ship. I needed to come, in person, to see the damage. So I can face their families and tell them what we've learned."

I gazed at him, noting the signs of strain, the white lines at his mouth and eye.

"And?" I prompted.

He shook his head. "I'm pleased you got the children when you did. Only moments later, it would have been disastrous." He closed his eyes and swallowed in concert. "The sheriff has explained all?"

Damien shook his head. "No. We have the children upstairs, and I've got my staff planning now."

I bit my lip, more than a little aware there was more to learn, but the terror that streaked through me warned me I may not like what I'd hear.

Andrew grunted. "I see. I sent a communiqué to the sheriff yesterday when I received news of the incident. He went down to the site, to see for himself what there was to find."

I glanced Damien's way. He shrugged, but there was a wealth of worry about the action.

"And?" Once more I prompted for information from my brother.

"It was an explosion. You could see the trajectory of the flames. It radiated from the centre, like the bloom of a flower." He rubbed at his brow.

Damien nodded. "I'd agree. My men and I looked for survivors. We found none. What we located, though, was this." From his pocket, he drew what appeared to be cogs, lots of small-sized discs.

"What are they?" I peered closer.

"Prong wheels used in replacement limbs. They make the musculature systems work." He pantomimed his arm moving up and down.

"They're special cogs manufactured from copper. Each is marked with a symbol, ensuring we know they were used by which physiotraducere."

I'd heard that word before and searched my memory. "Your mother was one, a specialist in the field, wasn't she?"

"Yes." The single-word answer was stark in the sudden quiet.

I bit my lip, unsure what this had to do with me, the children, or anything else. Then it occurred to me that that was my current state of affairs with everything.

Andrew grunted. "Each part used is numbered. The sheriff has his mother's records. We were checking them and found this part was used in the replacement of a leg. By a runaway from Haven."

Now my gut clenched. *Here* was a connection. "Who?"

Andrew shook his head. "I doubt you'd know him. Gerald Fansom."

The name didn't bring any people to mind. "No, you're right. I don't know the name." I looked at Damien, who also shook his head.

A sneer broke over Andrew's face. "I knew him slightly. He was in the outer circles of the Haven sect. An enforcer type of person. Someone you likely wouldn't have come in contact with at Haven House. He was *unclean*."

That meant he wasn't considered worthy of a formal position within the sect. Wouldn't be gifted with wives and a household of note, like those who were *worthy* did.

Andrew sighed. "I need to dig some more, and that means returning home. Leaving you here." Disquiet coloured his features, and I understood he was concerned about me. For me.

"D—" I gulped, unwilling to share any of the personal drawing I felt to the man watching me so intently. "The sheriff and I are preparing for whatever is needed. The children will be safe here, Andrew. I promise my life on that."

I didn't miss the tiny flicker at my misspoken word, though he winced at the last promise I made. His mouth tightened, and I could almost swear he'd snarl if he knew about our interlude from previously. "I would rather you were home with me. But you and the children are endangered right now. We need to know more, but the sheriff will keep you safe. He knows how and where." He bit the words out as he rose.

My gut curled, because while he was my brother, what was between Damien and myself—or may be at some unknown point in the future—was between us. Nothing to do with Andrew.

I watched Andrew pin Damien with a direct look of anger. Banked but noticeable. "Sheriff, if I may have a moment with my sister?"

Now my nerves danced and jumped faster and wilder.

Damien gave a tight nod and left the room. Andrew waited until the door closed behind him with a snap, then whirled back to face me. "What's happening here, Ammy?"

I almost sighed. Unused as I was to my brother being involved, it felt odd to explain my actions and emotions. "Nothing that is inappropriate, Andrew." I kept the words low and soothing, just as I'd done during my years at Haven House.

He merely quirked an eyebrow at me. "Define inappropriate."

"Andrew, don't ask me these questions," I entreated while tears pricked my eyes and fear danced along nerve endings.

His face deepened to a ruddy glow, but he kept his distance. His only physical reaction was the curling of his fists, a sign I didn't miss. "He's made advances?"

I squeaked. "No. But if he did, and I wanted it, that would be a matter for us to decide. Between ourselves, Andrew. Did anyone ask these questions of you with Gloriana?" I bit my lip, afraid I'd pushed too far. In Haven House, that would have drawn an immediate and physical punishment.

He jerked back, as if stung. "No! No, because neither of us—" In his face, I read sorrow and the need for forgiveness.

I reached out, took his hand. "Nothing inappropriate will happen. If something we want to happen does, or if I need help, I'll ask. But I've been kept in a cage for so long, I don't know what I want, Andrew. The sheriff—" I inhaled, hoping he'd understand my plea. "*Damien* is making no demands on me. Please, let it be, brother."

Anxiety bit at me, chomping deep until he gave a jerking nod of acceptance.

"Very well. For now I won't enquire. If you need me, ask. If you can't or don't feel comfortable, then talk to Gloriana. She will have an understanding."

How embarrassing! "Yes, if I need advice or assistance, I will let you know. Now, how long are you planning to stay? Should I have preparations made for dinner?"

The incredulous look he slanted at me did little to settle my fears. "No. I'm to leave immediately."

Andrew wound his arms around me and held me tight, and tears pricked my eyelids once more. "Be safe, Ammy. Be well and happy. It's all I ask." His voice carried a gravelly quality, and I blinked.

"I'm doing my best, Andrew." Whether that was enough, I couldn't say. All I knew was I'd fight for what felt right.

On that, he left the room. I watched his retreating back, then slumped into a chair as the door closed behind him.

I felt exhausted, terrified, and more than a little furious too.

Chapter Eight

I waited until Damien had walked Andrew to the door and seen him off, using the time to calm myself for the conversation ahead.

When Damien re-entered the room, I was ready. At least I thought so, but the grimness of his visage had that bravado melting like snow in summer. "What don't I know, Damien?"

For a moment, the shadows filling his eyes disappeared, and the lines at the sides of his eyes crinkled with his smile. "You have no idea how I feel when you use my name, Ammy."

I probably did, if it was anything like the sensations that plagued me. Had someone filled my veins with warm, gooey chocolate? I was sure they must have, because it drugged me, left my body strangely boneless.

He reached out a hand, and I took it. He pulled me closer, so I was buried in his arms and able to inhale the manly scent of him.

When his fingers burrowed under my chin and gently, yet irrevocably, urged it up, I was ready for his kiss. It was soft, like the kiss of a butterfly's wing. The heat and essence of him flowing over my skin was a drug I needed more of, while the pit in my centre warmed and unfurled.

The pressure of his lips on mine deepened so my mouth opened.

The tip of his tongue lapped at my lips, then slid within, and I moaned as his arms wrapped around me, hauling me closer so I could feel the hard planes of his body against mine through the layers of clothing.

My fingers inched upward, as if following some direction from my brain I knew nothing of. They coiled in the dark silky hair at the nape of his neck.

On a groan, Damien pulled away. "This is just the beginning, Ammy. One day, when you're ready, I'll show you more. The pleasure and the warmth of loving. I'll prove to you that you can remain independent and yet be part of what we have between us. That's my promise to you."

If only I could push beyond the barriers of my fears!

I moved back, unsteady without his support, when his hands fell away. I slid down into the nearest chair.

"Later. Danger. Tell me about it," I whispered.

"It's deep. We've got the enforcer from Haven, or at least some part of his leg. We've got the children and a threat to you. The dirigible is destroyed and lives lost. We've been followed and tracked, and there are not a lot of leads at this point. I know it has to do with the sect but can't see how the pieces fit together yet." In his voice lay a wealth of disgust. At himself?

"You're doing everything you can—"

"It's not enough, Ammy. I'm missing some vital clue and don't even know where to begin. I brought you here because Andrew was sure they'd try to reclaim you. We promised a haven to the children's mother, and with Letitia failing, we've acted on that. I just don't see where the connection is. I should be able to see it."

I watched his face, the play of emotions. His hands moved as he made his points and tried to see what he could. "You know who their father is?"

"Francesca is the child of Letitia and Reverend Cunningham. It was a love match from all I can glean. Then when he died, she was *reapportioned*." Her gut churned when Damien used the term Master and Junior had always used to describe what happened to the widows and children upon the passing of a man within the sect.

"I know about reapportionment, and I believe it's inhuman. I saw a new wife brought in from that. She was barely seventeen with two children and expecting a third when she joined the household. Junior didn't care and took her as a wife. He declared the children unclean and sent them away. I don't honestly know what he did with them." I shuddered, remembering the screams of children and mother. A hard-faced woman dragging them into a carriage and away. The girl had miscarried three days later.

I dragged my hands over her mouth at the memory.

"Ammy?"

I shook my head. How could I possibly explain the things I'd seen and heard? "I can't. Please, Damien. Some things are too much to remember." Hot tears dribbled down my face.

"One day, you'll tell me, and we'll make sure they face justice. Together." His words fell on me like a warm balm, and I dipped my head so he wouldn't see just how much that promise meant to me. I'd been alone so long that the words didn't so much confuse me as weaken my resistance to him. I may have given in to touches and kisses, but more? Well, if that happened, it was a long way off.

"Ammy?" I heard the concern.

"I'm fine. But how does all this mean we may need to evacuate?" Then I decided I really should kick myself, because hadn't they already blown up the dirigible? Maybe his home and his staff were now in danger. My head snapped up, and I narrowed my eyes. "I've brought the threat here, haven't I?"

He didn't refute my words. "They've been outside the gates since a couple nights ago. They're automatons."

I frowned. "How do you know that? What does this mean for us?"

"I recognise some of the faces. I went upstairs and scanned the perimeter with my ocular."

I frowned. "Ocular? What's that?"

"It's an object for seeing into the distance. Usually used on either a dirigible or seagoing vessel, but free-standing with both legs and dual eyepieces. I had one installed some time back, but this is the first time it's been employed in protection of the house."

Didn't that impress on me just what I'd brought with me? "So, you know some. You've garnered their background, I imagine?"

He shrugged. "I've had previous experience with one or two *indi-*

viduals lining the gates. It's why I believe we should evacuate now. There're at least forty people currently watching us. They're dangerous and armed. I noted the bandoliers some are wearing."

"So we run. Where to?"

He smiled. "Somewhere far away. I've already been in contact with one of my trusted allies, and we leave tonight. Under the cover of darkness."

"But Andrew..." I gulped.

"He knows I have many connections. He trusts me to keep you safe, Ammy."

"Running isn't the answer, Damien."

He shook his head. "Not normally, but until we know why, there's no further choice. The threads of evil run deep. You're the key, it seems, but we don't know why. We keep you and the children safe until we can fight, Ammy."

Guilt rode me hard as I rose. "So, we'll take the carriage tonight."

"No carriage. We leave on foot for the first part. Pack only what's important and some clothing. The rest will be taken care of. I'll come when darkness falls, Ammy. Have the children ready."

I blinked. "Of course." I walked to the door, but he followed and stopped me.

"This isn't your fault."

He could say that for eternity, but if I was the key, it *was* my fault. That knowledge was totally unacceptable, and I'd do everything I could to make things right once more.

Night fell, and we moved down the servants' staircase. I carried Constance while Francesca carried Faith. Damien had dragooned Simeon into keeping track of Samson. Jessie, Frank—who would act as one of our guards—and Aloysius, the other guard, carried the rucksacks at the back of the snaking line. The house had been locked down, as it had been every night.

Damien had called the staff together as we waited. "Thank you for joining us. As you can see, we are evacuating. This should ensure your safety as much as ours. Should the house be breached, your protection is far more important than this residence. Jerome has the authority to handle things to do with the household on my behalf. He does not know where we're going, for everyone's safety."

I understood why he'd said that. If someone tried to find out from the staff, they could honestly say they didn't know where we'd be. Clearly he had a plan, though he hadn't shared it with me at this point.

"Let me repeat, your safety above this house. There is nothing here that will lead anyone to where we'll be sheltering, but I will be watching and aware. For now, I bid you all adieu."

The doors to the drawing room, where he'd instructed them all to gather, were shut by Jerome, who followed us down the hall toward where I imagined the kitchens lay.

We moved down the stairs leading to the basement. The illumination of the ionic gas lanterns the adults carried was small but effective, lighting our way. At the bottom of the steps, Jerome turned right, toward the wall, and shoved at an elaborate carving, revealing a keyhole. From the pocket of his waistcoat, he produced a large, gnarly key and inserted it. The lock ground but gave, and a door swung open.

The tiny lamp in my hand illuminated the passage beyond just enough that I could make out steps and handholds. With trepidation, I stepped within, Francesca and the boys following. I waited as Damien retrieved the key from Jerome's hand. They embraced, and a manly patting ensued as a draft invaded this dim and cavernous passage.

"Stay safe, old friend," Jerome muttered, then stepped back. The others entered the now crowded area, and Damien turned the key before turning back to me.

"We should hurry. We've a long way to go before we meet our conveyance."

I hugged Constance closer, pleased she'd snuggled down in the blanket I'd wrapped around her. Jessie, Francesca, and I had dressed the children warmly, ensuring their clothes and shoes were sensible, and I'd done the same for myself. Still, that sneaky chill burrowed into my bones, and I shivered. What we'd find, come the end of the night, I had no idea. I just hoped there was warm food and a comfortable bed waiting for me.

Damien moved to the front, the boys following, while Francesca, Jessie, and I moved into the centre with the men at our back. I felt the weight of the pistol on my hip. Damien had been insistent that both Francesca and I be armed. Not that either of us had any experience with such items, but he'd argued that we might be separated. That had been enough to end my complaints against arming us.

We moved in relative silence, only the sounds of footfalls and the occasional grump from the children filling the air. We walked and walked for what felt like hours until he raised a hand.

An opening lay ahead, a metal grate overgrown with vines. "Extinguish your lights."

We followed his instructions while he searched his pocket for a small circlet of keys. He tried several with quiet cursing until one slid within and the gate opened. "Stay here until I call you forward."

I watched as he slipped through the opening, disappearing from sight. Long, agonising moments passed, and then he returned, urging us forward. "Be quick but silent. Not a word."

We followed him forward toward a conveyance the likes of which I'd never seen before. He handed us into the rear of the covered wagon, stinking of something I refused to consider. On the side, I'd caught sight of "Night Soil" emblazoned in red and green. Within was a single long bench. I urged the children, men, and Jessie to take a seat, leaving room at the front for myself and the rear for Damien, once he'd climbed aboard.

One child gagged, and I moved forward, shushing them as Damien disappeared for several long moments, my guts squeezing hard with fear. When he reappeared, he clambered inside. The door shut behind us with a clang.

"Shh," he reminded us all, finger to his lips.

He motioned me forward to the front, where he showed me a sliding window, tiny but enough that he and I could spy on where we were. He tapped the panel between us and the driver, and the vehicle rumbled forward with an odd sway.

We passed the mansion, and I noted the crowd had grown. I looked at Damien, whose face turned grim. On and on we travelled. I moved to the bench and sat down. Constance settled on my lap, thumb in her mouth as she slept in my embrace.

By the time the sun was rising in the sky, Francesca was dozing against Jessie, and the boys had settled against the shoulders of the two men beside them.

Weariness battered me, and I hoped we wouldn't be travelling much longer when suddenly we stopped.

The sound of birds, their long cries, and the odd watery sound filled my mind.

"Where are we?"

"Wait and see," Damien offered, and when I looked at him, I could see some of the tension had eased from his features.

Once more, the scraping clang filled the air, and the fresh oxygen chased away the stuffy stink we'd endured for a long while.

Damien was the first out, the men following suit and handing the children down, then reaching out for the bags they dropped to their feet.

When I reached Damien, Aloysius took Constance from my grasp, the child murmuring in her sleep as he held her against his body. Damien took me in his grip, strong fingers spanning my waist as he lifted me and slid my body down his. For a moment, a hint of that magic assailed me. Once on the ground, I stepped away from him, refusing to let anyone question what lay between us.

In the distance, an azure blue filled my gaze. Nearer to me lay sand. "The ocean?" A large vessel rested at anchor, and I gasped. "We're going on a ship?"

Damien's lips quirked up. "Yes. Now we need to get down to the beach, so grab Constance."

Aloysius handed the child back to me. Then he and Frank hefted the bags while the sleepy children groused. We stumbled and lumbered toward the shore. Three rowboats waited, and seamen hurried to help us into the tiny vessels. Damien settled beside me, and the rhythm of the men's strokes had us moving swiftly away from the shore.

"How did you arrange all of this so quickly?" I glanced at him. He smiled but didn't answer.

The soft breeze caressed my skin, and exhaustion settled in, making me heavy and relaxed.

At the side of the ship, the seamen grabbed ropes and tied the tiny boats. One man took Constance and, in a feat of athleticism, climbed the side of the ship with her in his very firm grasp. Another assisted Faith while I watched, heart in my throat the entire time. Only when they were safely over the side of the vessel did I breathe again. The boys climbed up like small monkeys. Then Francesca and I were urged to go next. Frank moved in behind the young girl and Damien behind me. The bite of the rope hurt my hands, but I refused to be assisted.

"You're doing excellently, Miss Francesca," I heard Frank urging her, while she moaned as if about to be nauseous.

Refusing to show any weakness, I swallowed back the instinctive urge to vomit and climbed, gaze set to the top.

A hand reached down, grasped my wrist as I reached the top, and assisted me over the side. I'd never been so pleased to be on a solid surface, and I waited for Damien to join me. The children were ushered below by Jessie, who'd been followed by Aloysius, and while they muttered and complained, I was thankful that for a short while, the responsibility wasn't mine.

Damien grasped my hand and dragged me toward the captain.

"Sheriff, when I received your message, I was thankful we were barely a day's sailing from here," the captain said. "We'll raise anchor once the dinghies are raised and secured."

At that I heard sounds of exertion, grunts, and the squeaking of wheels. I turned to watch as suddenly the small wooden craft rose over the side and up onto odd-looking metal stands. Men called and climbed, rather like an exotic ballet of movement while they secured the tiny boats in place. Once the task was completed, they moved away from view, and I turned back to note the captain had left.

Damien's gaze had settled on me with a smile. "I take it you've never sailed?"

"No. Haven wasn't a place with ocean views, and we were confined to the house and grounds," I answered.

He released my hand, and I felt bereft until his arm wound around my shoulders.

"Come, we should go below. You'll want to wash and change. Jessie will attend to your clothes later, but you'll need some food before you rest."

At his words, the overwhelming urge for slumber rose. "I could sleep."

"Trust me, you'll wish to bathe," he said with a laugh.

I sniffed the air and almost gagged. "Of course. You're right. Take me where I need to be."

Damien led the way and opened a door at the end of the corridor. "This will be your cabin, Ammy."

It was small, compact really, but there was a tub waiting for me. I turned to thank him, but he was already shutting the door behind me.

On a sigh, I stripped down and slid into the tub. Thoughtfully, they'd left soap and a dish so I could wash my hair. I scrubbed and rinsed until I was sure no trace of the scent was left on me. The satchel I'd carried sat on the floor, and I slipped from the tub, towel wound around me, and crouched down, opening it.

Once dressed, I sighed. I might be clean, but the clothes I'd removed stank like an outhouse. "Oh, don't be precious, Amaryllis."

I headed for the door, aware that during my bath, we must have set sail, as the ship now had a steady rocking movement. Soothing, and not the least nauseating. I smiled. "I'm on a boat." I'd dreamed about that during those long years at Haven House. Another dream come true, along with my wish to leave that house.

I hurried from the cabin, retracing my steps to the deck. I glanced around and stopped. On the front of the ship, there was a screen which obscured my view somewhat. But I could see feet and a head. Damien's.

He was washing beyond the screen, and the sight of him, those long legs with water sluicing over him, stilled me. The heat I associated with his nearness turned into a raging firestorm inside my body.

In that moment, I couldn't lie to myself. I wasn't just drawn to this man. I yearned for him. The touch and promises he'd made to me were the tip of the enchantment, and it wound around me. It was more. Bigger. Because I lusted for him too.

Desire ran through my veins like quicksilver.

I couldn't live in a place like Haven House and be unaware of physical desire and lust. It had permeated every inch of the house.

For the first time, I acknowledged it was what I now felt. For Damien.

Rooted to the spot, I watched as he turned, tipping the bucket over him.

The instant he saw me, I knew. His eyes turned smoky green, and the planes of his face tensed. "Ammy."

That was all it took to have me taking a step forward. Then another. Closer to what I knew I needed, like fresh air in my lungs.

"Damien."

I'd almost reached him when another voice called, "Sheriff, I—"

I turned, spying the captain where he'd stopped his forward motion, his eyes taking in the tableau before him. I knew exactly what he saw.

A woman—a very forward woman—ogling the man I knew to be naked and bathing behind the screen. A woman someplace she had no right to be.

Oh my God! He'll think I'm not just fast but also loose.

Heat burned across my cheeks. I'd been discovered about to take part in something forbidden. An unmarried woman—and a man she wasn't even affianced to—in a compromising situation!

I glanced down and caught sight of Damien's bare feet, and once more, awareness of just how much of a fool I was slammed into me. Gulping didn't help, and neither did the hot tide washing over my face, neck, and chest. The blush was a complete giveaway.

"I didn't mean to intrude," I mumbled, then fled down the corridor and back to my cabin.

Chapter Nine

I didn't join anyone for breakfast; instead, I stayed in the cabin and tried to sleep. Facing anyone at this point was too much. Damien may have come and knocked on my door—I was fairly sure it was him, as the lock rattled and I heard someone calling, muffled though it was by the pillow over my head. I'd have to face him later, because hiding wasn't really me. After all, there weren't many places to hide on a ship, were there?

I knew the children would be fine. After all, Jessie was there, so I let myself be, drifting finally as exhaustion overcame me. At some point I must have dozed off, because waking—groggy and cold—I could see the sun was sitting on the horizon.

I moved my stiff limbs, used the small privy in the corner, and washed my face in the dish, the water cool.

Brushing my hair, I gazed at myself in the mirror. I would never call myself beautiful, though handsome might suit. Raven-black hair, deep violet-coloured eyes, and fine features. My lips weren't full. In fact, some might call them thin, but they were a deep rosy red. With my hair returned to the ordered bun at the back of my head, my plain dark green gown smoothed down, I knew procrastinating further wouldn't help the situation.

I grasped the knob and opened the door before I could talk myself out of it.

The creak and groan of the metal panels didn't bother me as I climbed the wooden stairs to the deck and the sea air, enervating and stronger than usual, wafted over me.

Just as I placed a foot on the deck, a voice called to me. "Miss Amaryllis, the sheriff asked me to let you know he wishes to see you in the captain's office."

I turned to note Aloysius striding toward me. He was a big man, his skin glittering bronze in the fading light. He also had received at least one replacement that I could make out, his gait heavy and slightly lopsided. I'd need to learn his story at some point.

"Of course, Aloysius. If you could direct me to the office?"

He smiled, thick lips widening and his eyes glinting. "This way."

He motioned to the side of the ship, and I followed him. A hidden door opened wide to admit us, and up a staircase we went. "This ship is quite large. Has the sheriff owned it long?"

"The sheriff don't own it. At least, not as the sheriff. It belongs to the corporation, Miss Amaryllis."

"The corporation," I parroted.

"Oh yes. His mama done started a business when his daddy died. She weren't just a physiotraducere, but she also owned the business that makes the cogs. It's why he knew where to find the number."

I stopped still, and Aloysius turned and smiled. "Don't feel bad, Miss Amaryllis. He don't make much of the money he has, and he gives lots away to help those in need. He helps seed companies and organizations what help others. Pays for medications and surgeries too. Even put my sister Kalani through medical school so she could become a physiotraducere. She worked for him while she studied and is now in her own clinic."

I bit my lip. He was a philanthropist of note, then. "So why does he...?" I waved my hand, and Aloysius smiled.

"You'll have to ask him yourself, Miss Amaryllis."

"Ammy," I corrected him. "Call me Ammy."

He shook his head. "Nah-ah. I ain't doing that. Miss Ammy is the best I can do."

I smiled. "Then Miss Ammy will do. Thanks, Aloysius."

He pushed the door open, and I stepped inside an office of gleaming copper and wood, and the door shut behind me.

Damien—*the sheriff*, I told myself, hoping to ward off the lust that simmered inside me—waited at the desk, his eyes shadowed with fatigue, like dark smudges. "Ammy, you slept?"

"A little," I replied and stepped closer. "You didn't."

He spread his hands over the desk. "Too much to do. Too many questions and not enough answers."

I took his words as an invitation and settled into the seat opposite him. "I'm so sorry about earlier."

"Why?" He tilted his head to the side, gazing at me with a strange intensity.

"I... You were bathing. It was unseemly and wrong of me." The only problem with my words was I wasn't sorry. Or not completely. That confused me. "But we should talk about—"

He rose. "Stop, Ammy."

I stared at him as he prowled toward me.

"You liked what you saw." It wasn't a question, and my mouth dried at what he inferred.

"I... It was wrong," I whispered. Lying fixed nothing, and I wanted —needed—to sidestep the question.

"Ammy, you liked what you saw. Yes or no?"

I gulped. "I... Yes." The word was dragged from somewhere deep inside me.

He reached out, took my hand, and raised me up so I was flat against him.

"Good. If the captain hadn't come by, we would have done more. You know that, don't you?"

"Yes."

"You want what's between us, the same as I do. I know you're confused. I know we have much to concentrate on, Ammy. Never be embarrassed, though," he whispered against my cheek, and I shivered with anticipation of the kiss I knew was coming.

The touch of breath against skin was enervating, and I closed my eyes as I felt him lower his head, then touch his lips against mine. The kiss was dark, carnal, and hungry as fingers dug into skin through the layers of clothing. It wasn't enough. I yearned for more, but as quickly as the kiss began, he tugged away. I opened my heavy lids and watched him. His own eyes were slumberous.

"We'll do more soon, Ammy." Damien caressed my cheek before stepping away, keeping hold of my hand. He led me to the chair beside him, and I sank down before he settled in his own. "We have the records my mother kept."

That tweaked something in my mind. "Your mother. She made the parts?"

He laughed. "Not herself, but yes, she built the business that manufactures the replacement limbs."

"Why? Why would a woman who trained as a physiotraducere want to create the parts herself?"

"Because she could never get what she needed. Too many manufacturing companies refused to deal with a woman. They would short the orders, or they'd be the leftovers. My mother took pride in her work. In the end, she came up with ideas to not just streamline her work but to improve the products. Her clients—public and private—were always given the best of her abilities. She and I were both proud of what she achieved."

I nodded, now that I could understand the reasoning behind her strange choice. "She did well."

Damien nodded. "The other surgeons used her equipment, and word spread. It meant expanding her manufactory. More men and women employed. More time to do what she wanted when she wasn't working for the government. Greater profits. She did, however, insist on keeping exact records. Where every piece went. It was part of the agreements she reached with the organisations she supplied, ensuring she received details of every part used."

This all seemed odd. "Why did she keep the records?"

"Mother walked a fine line. She felt her skills should be kept for those who needed them, not just the wealthy or those with the muscle to hurt. I believe it was along the lines of if one of her patients abused the power and strength that came with the implants, then she could find her notes. Tell what she'd done. Why. If by some chance she was duped, then she'd know by whom."

I digested his words in silence. She'd done everything she could to safeguard herself in a man's world.

"The parts you found?"

"I traced the numbers. It's not good news, Ammy. They were used on a Haven man, as I told you. An enforcer. We know who paid for the work, and the physician involved."

The gravity of his words had me frowning.

"And?"

"We only know the basics. The surgery was paid for by the Haven House Trust. Ammy, who has access to those funds?"

Scrunching my nose, I fought with my memory. *Haven House Trust.* I couldn't place it, though there was a familiarity about it.

"Ammy?"

"I don't remember." It was the truth. With some time, I might remember, but...

"It's okay," he said and covered my hand with his. It was warm and soothed me unlike anything else.

"You've checked the manifest of the dirigible?"

Damien grimaced. "Apparently it's missing. Andrew and I spoke of that before you entered the room. The only copies were on the dirigible and are now destroyed."

"Oh."

"Yes." He scratched at the back of his neck. "If only I had some way of keeping track of what we know."

Once more, I bit my lip. "It's too bad you don't have a schoolroom blackboard. You could—"

Damien rose. "Of course! That's it."

I watched, lost at the sudden exultation on his face.

"What?"

"We have one—well, actually several—on the ship. I think, anyway." He scratched his head, grabbed a sheaf of papers on the left of the desk, and flicked through pages. "Yes. They were being sent to a school as part of our philanthropic program. All I need to do is give the captain the direction and have it brought up here. You're a brilliant woman, Amaryllis."

That made me feel rather uncomfortable, as I hadn't really done anything spectacular. While I tried to consider how to tell him that, he pressed a button on the radioscope. I heard him ask the captain to find and deliver the blackboard; then he rose and moved toward me. "You look exhausted. Let me arrange a cup of tea."

He opened a cupboard behind him, revealing a large kettle resting on a heater plate, then a second cupboard that contained cups and a teapot.

He moved assuredly, setting everything out on a tray before bringing it back to the desk.

"You're incredibly handy there, Damien," I muttered as he placed the tray on the wood top.

"You'd be surprised just what I can do. Remember, my mother and I were alone for a long time. After my father passed, well, I had to learn quickly." He settled at the desk and poured the tea into fragile cups. "Mother... Let's just say I had to assist her in the early days. When things improved, we still did a lot for ourselves, because she always said we should never expect others to do for us what we have the time and skills to undertake ourselves. One never forgets skills like these, and when I'm on location, I don't have people with me to attend to my needs. I prefer it that way, though."

Every admission revealed more of the complexities of this man. It made me want him more. Something I was quickly coming to understand wasn't just about the baser and carnal urges so much as the qualities he hid from sight.

I drank my tea in silence, digesting all he'd said. As we finished, a knock came from behind me, and I startled.

"That will be the blackboard," Damien told me as he rose to open the door.

A large sheet of slate, mounted on a wooden surround, was carried inside by four sailors, puffing and panting with exertion. "Cap'n said you'd be wanting this too."

The oldest man held out a box, and when Damien opened it, his face crinkled into a smile. "Excellent," he muttered as he pulled a heavy blackboard duster and chalk from within.

"Cap'n also said dinner will be in the dining room in an hour." The men quickly filed from the room, and the door shut behind them.

I stood there, teacup in my hand still.

"So, Ammy, let's write down what we know." He set to work, white chalk marking the board.

Haven. My background summed up succinctly: "Bought from father, rescued by brother." He wrote the names of my five charges on the board, the name of the man whose enhancements had been found after the explosion—Gerald Fansom—and in the centre of everything sat one word: Haven.

"It's not a lot," I said, staring at the slate.

"No. But more will come. I've got people, including Andrew, looking for clues. I sent him Fansom's details, or the bit I had. It's not much either, but at least a name will allow us to start."

A *ding* rang through the air, and he muttered, pushing papers aside and opening a cupboard. A mechanical monstrosity filled the cavern.

"What's that?"

He smiled, though it was cold and remote. "It's a communicase. Allows me to remain in contact with friends via secure wireless transmission."

I blinked. "Wireless transmission?"

"It allows me to send and receive messages. I can't 'speak' or 'hear' as transmission is only the written word." He flicked switches and turned a dial, and a long paper extruded from the device. He scanned it, frowned, and passed it to me.

Gerard Fansom was a member of Haven's security detail. On the outside of the ring. He's been missing for four days, along with several high-ranking officials. Master and Junior are also missing. As soon as I have more, I'll report back in. Keep my sister safe. AC.

. . .

I wasn't sure how to take this missive. After all, I wasn't just an adult but also a person capable of free thought and movement. The knowledge that Andrew thought I needed to be protected irked me for a moment. Then reality intruded. To be fair, this was a situation I was highly unprepared for.

"We should head down to the dining room. Dinner will be served soon, and we should look in on the children too."

His words brought me back to my responsibilities, and I gasped.

"Oh my, yes!" I'd almost forgotten them while helping Damien. "I'm sure they're fine." Now I bit my lip, feeling as if I'd completely abandoned them. "Jessie was with them, as was Francesca, but it's not fair that they had to care for them all day." Heat radiated from my cheeks. I tugged up my skirts and headed to the door I'd entered through.

"No, this way is easiest," Damien offered, and I took his outstretched hand. The connection between us was warm, like a sizzle of awareness.

We hurried down the stairs, and by the time Damien had squired me to the cabin door, I had no idea where I was.

"It's okay. You'll find your way around here soon enough."

The door opened, and I noted with surprise the spaciousness of their quarters. Three rooms opened to a large communal space.

"I gave the captain orders to ensure they were put into a suite," Damien explained. "He had it ready for them."

Constance and Faith were snuggled up with Francesca on a lounge chair as she read to them. They had that sleepy, content look, while the two boys settled in with some blocks, and Jessie cleared a table. Clearly they'd already eaten.

Francesca laid the book down and looked at me. Once more I felt that sliver of unease, that somehow I'd failed. "We're fine," she murmured in a tone that soothed. "We've kept busy today, and the girls will retire soon."

"I'll come down tomorrow morning. Maybe we could..." I bit my lip. What could I possibly have the skills to assist with? "What do you need for the boys?"

Francesca slanted me with a look far more worldly than a girl of her age should use. As if she were ten years older than her biological age. "They need schooling. Education."

My mind blanked, but then I whirled, looking at Damien. "The things you have in the hold. Are there books? Primers and slates?"

He nodded.

"If I could have some for the boys. I might work with them." Here was what I needed to be useful. "I can work with them in the morning, if that's acceptable, Francesca. Now for you..."

She shook her head. "I'll look after the little ones and sew."

"But what about your education?"

The glance she threw at me was yearning, which quickly disappeared, followed by a mask of indifference. "I'm a girl. Education isn't for me. Or at least more than a basic one and according to the elders, I've got more than enough."

Fury ignited within me, but before I could speak, Damien answered. "That's not right, Francesca. Your education is vitally important. Once we deal with this issue, I'll engage a tutor for all of you. If you want an education, it will be made available."

The girl blinked, her eyes shining like jewels. "I... Thank you, Sheriff."

A sound echoed through the ship. I turned to Damien. "What was that?"

"The dinner hour. Come, we need to meet the captain in the dining room."

He ushered me away, his hand on my arm nearly burning through the length of my dark sleeve.

Chapter Ten

I entered the children's suite, hoping for books and perhaps slate. What I found were some desks, two new slates, a pile of books, and even a writing book.

The books ranged from primers to encyclopaedias. I shook my head as Jessie smiled. "They passed a quiet night. None of the younger ones woke at all, and Miss Faith only once went to use the lavatory."

"All right, then. You prepare them, then rest. Francesca and I can take over. You can take the afternoon and night duties, if that suits you."

"Yes, Miss Ammy." She retreated, and moments later, Simeon and Samson entered the room.

Jessie ushered them to the table in the corner, and I settled into the luxurious armchair and scanned the books. Where to start? Perhaps I needed to find out what education they'd had.

Calling Francesca forward, I waited as the girl took the seat beside me. "What schooling have the boys had?"

Francesca's lips thinned. "Not enough. They can read. Simeon more than Samson, as Mama started before she got ill. Samson can form letters and knows their sounds, but that's about all. I would have taken over, but with four…" She shrugged. "Mama's illness was long and difficult. It took a lot of time, so I couldn't spend it with them."

They'd had a horrible time, and I felt the guilt eating at me. How could I improve her lot in life? "You like to sew?"

She nodded. "I'm good at it too."

She might be good, but it clearly didn't fill the yearning inside. She had that look of someone who was resigned to something she didn't want to do. "If you could choose to be anything, what would it be?"

A glint lit in her eyes. "Anything?"

"Yes, Francesca. Anything."

"A physician. Someone with the power to heal. Someone who can make the sick better."

Reaching out, I clasped Francesca's hand, felt the subtle tightening. "You wish you could have been there for your mother?" It didn't seem like magic to work that out.

She nodded. "None would come at first. The doctor said she'd get better, and besides, she'd have done better if she'd stayed with her husband. He was no husband, Miss Amaryllis. No father. He simply bedded her." Vitriol spewed forth, something I knew well, and my gut knotted at her words.

"Then I'll talk to the sheriff. We'll get you tutors for science and math. If it can be done, you will become a doctor someday."

I knew she didn't believe me because her lips twisted. "You can't promise."

This was the time I could gain her trust. I wouldn't lie, because that wouldn't be in anyone's best interests. "If I can make it happen, I will. The sheriff wants you to be what and who you want to be. Not because some sick men made up rules for women that make no sense and keep us from being who we can be, but because it's what we're called to do."

A shiver wound its way through her. The urge to comfort and embrace the girl came and went. Ignoring it hurt me on an intense level, but instinctively I knew she wouldn't welcome it and wasn't ready.

"We'll see," she muttered and rose. Walking back to the others, she settled in to soothe the now-fretful Faith.

I studied them, five children ranging from almost adult to little more than a baby and wondered at how similar they were, yet different. Francesca was dark-haired, her long tresses confined in a tight braid. Her

Cupid's bow lips pink, eyes grey. Cheekbones that appeared chiselled. Slim. I could see why Letitia wanted her out of Haven now.

Samson and Simeon were dark-haired too, though it was a mass of frizzy, tight curls. Their eyes were the muddy green-brown of hazel. Freckles covered the bridges of their noses, and they were sturdy of body. Stout legs betrayed the running and carrying they'd done for their mother. Confinement wouldn't be easy for them.

The two youngest girls, with jet-black hair, frizzed and tightly curled. Skin fine with a mere dusting of freckles. They also shared what I guessed were features passed down through their paternal line.

Once the children had broken their fast, I called the boys over and settled them at the desks, then set tasks. I needed to see how much they knew. I had them read, something they showed a great aptitude toward. Writing was less successful. They knew letters and sounds, but they lacked other skills such as punctuation and grammar. Their mathematics were adequate.

By the time the midday meal came, they were tired of sitting and academic work, and I let them join their sisters at the table. Francesca's eyes, far too old and worldly, met mine. I knew what she wanted to know: Could I help them?

I settled myself at the table and watched the children eat slowly. The stew they'd been served was hearty and warming. Yet, while I read hunger in their faces, I wondered at the way they ate, as if savouring each bite.

The silence stretched as no one talked. At the end of the meal, Jessie appeared and bundled the children up. "I'll go up top and let them stretch their legs for a bit."

Assessing the boys, I caught her eyes. "Get one of the men, either Frank or Aloysius, to assist."

She smiled at me. "Yes, Miss Ammy."

Jessie hustled the four youngest from the room, and I turned to Francesca.

"Your brothers both have gaps in their learning."

"The school refused them, so I worked with them when opportunities came. They're good boys, but they *are* boys." She shrugged, and I wanted to laugh.

"Perhaps you should join us upstairs tonight when we dine. Do you have a clean gown?" I glanced down at her dusty three-quarter faded brown outfit.

"No. I had to make sure Constance and Faith had what they needed."

Unsure how to accept the fact that she'd taken on the role of pseudo-mother to the four younger children, I made a point of telling myself to check with Damien on whether they also carried cloth or clothing in the hold.

I rose and dusted off my skirts. "I'm going to my cabin to eat and wash. I'll return—"

"We'll be fine for the afternoon." She twined a strand of hair which had loosened from her braid around her finger. "Did you mean what you said?" Uncertainty appeared in her gaze, and she raised her chin. As if expecting me to say no, I gathered.

"About what?" I asked, keeping my tone gentle.

"Dinner. Joining you."

I smiled and reached out, stilling her hands. "Yes. I'll talk to the sheriff and arrange it. I'll also see what other clothing might be found for you."

She started, but I turned and left the suite, my feet retracing yesterday's path. At the room marked "Office," I knocked and then entered when Damien called to "Come."

He was sitting in the chair behind the desk, hair wild and jutting up in many directions. The urge to stomp forward and kiss him rose, heating me so I was sure my skin would split and some wild, wanton woman would emerge.

"Ammy." His tone carried a silky quality, and his eyes glinted. "Shut the door and come sit down."

He pointed to the chair opposite, and I detected a gleam of humour lurking in the depths. Could he tell what I was thinking?

Settling into the hardwood chair, I gave myself a moment, gazing at him. His face wasn't perfect. It was nicked and scarred at his chin, though it was firm. The dark hair framing his face, now released from the leather strap he usually controlled it with, flowed over his broad shoulders. His lips, firm and full, widened into a smile as I continued my slow perusal.

"Ammy?"

I raised my eyes so I could look into his. Those dark green pools offered me something I was afraid to accept. "I came... Uh, I want Francesca to join us as we dine. Also cloth. She needs clothes or cloth, as she didn't pack for herself."

His brows raised. "Why? You told her to."

Now that I was on firm ground, I leaned into my seat. "She said Constance and Faith needed more than a single change. She had to give up hers for them."

"I'll talk with the captain, then. I believe we had some clothing and bolts of cloth. Is there anything else you need for the children?"

I bit my lip and considered how to make the request. "Francesca wants... It seems her schooling was curtailed, and she's been working with the children. But she wants to be a doctor."

He cocked his head to one side. "I see. She'll need specialist tutors. Science, math, and so on."

I nodded. "Yes. But I fear she may also have other gaps in her education. When we're settled... Where are we going, anyway?"

Damien frowned. "I have some business interests in Port Alino. I've not yet made them public, but I have a house there. Smaller than home, but it would be suitable. I thought we'd make landfall there. Besides, I have the cargo to unload there."

"Where is Port Alino?" I'd never heard of it.

His smile grew broader. He reached for a map and beckoned me to join him behind the desk.

I rose and moved, squeaking when he grabbed my wrist and pulled me down to his lap.

I heard the whoosh of breath and the caress of his exhalation upon my skin. Dancing nerves took up the quiver that occurred every time we touched.

"Damien?" I half turned, and he groaned.

"If you look at me like that, Ammy, I'll have to kiss you." His voice took on a gravelly nature, and I shivered.

He tugged me closer until our lips touched. The kiss was gentle to begin with. Soft and feather-light. My lips opened beneath his urging, and the taste of him, dark and rich, filled me.

"Damien," I muttered, and he deepened the kiss. Boneless, I nestled closer, and the touch of his fingers digging into my skin through layers of clothing as he urged me on felt right.

My body heated, and I moaned, lifting my head. His lips traced a fiery path along my jaw and down my neck as I arched my back.

With a growl, he tugged away. Below me, I detected a distinct hardness.

"Damien?"

His chest bellowed, as did mine, the fever still present in my blood. "Let me say this once, Ammy. I want you. I would strip you naked and have my way with you here on the desk if I could. If you were willing and ready. But you aren't. I'll wait for that, and someday, you will be. But I am a man, Ammy. Your nearness feeds the beast inside me. Makes me want you and forever. What's between us is more than simple lust."

I couldn't look away, the connection between us pulsing with excitement.

The words shocked me, because he'd never pushed this hard before. It both scared and surprised me. What did I want? The question ate at me.

He sighed and shook his head. "You aren't ready, so I'll wait. Now, Port Alino."

The change of subject surprised me. He dragged the map closer and pointed at it. "Here. It's a small community on the coastline, fishing and cloth manufacturing. They're also building a new facility for the manufacturing and distillation of apothecarists' decoctions based on natural elements found locally."

"Medical supplies?" I blinked, amazed at what he was proposing.

His smile melted away. "Many of the medications in general use are based on synthetics and owned by the Igneous Corporation. The costs are astronomical, as no one else competes against them. That puts them out of the reach of common men and women. I've brought distillation artificers to Port Alino. Masters in the field. We need adequate supplies before we can approach the health committees about replacing the lesser items with ours. Lower cost, better quality."

"And you propose we base ourselves there until you have more information?"

"Yes."

At his elbow came an imperious ping. Our heads swivelled. "My communicase."

I stood and moved to the side as he reached out and pulled the tape toward him, then scanned it.

Who is the missing girl from Haven? We might have our first clear break. AC.

Andrew had asked for information I could easily give him. Except I didn't want to. It was like every aspect of my life was tainted by the time in that place.

I just want to forget about it and be normal again!

Damien's gaze captured mine. "Do you know the missing woman Andrew is enquiring about?"

I nodded, my mind wanting to shy away from what I'd seen that night. "Eldora. She was a newer wife. Came from outside Haven. Junior had to travel as there was some sort of agreement." I willed myself to remember those details without the scent of copper and the scarlet ribbons of fluid I'd seen. There'd been so much, and even now, my stomach threatened to evacuate what was within.

"Ammy?" Damien was up immediately, winding his arms around me.

I leaned in, needing the strength and support he offered. "He killed her. At least I think he did." The memories wouldn't go away. They washed over me, heating and then chilling me to my marrow at the same time. "There was so much blood. She was never seen again."

Rivers of fluid streamed down my face, and I hid my head in his chest, needing what he wordlessly gave me. I gripped the sleeves of his jacket, hands numb against the chill I couldn't will away.

"I'm sorry, Ammy. I know it's hard, but I need to know what you remember. Tell me everything."

My stomach roiled at the request, and I gulped. "I don't want to," I choked out while my eyes remained squeezed shut. It didn't chase away what I'd seen. It was as if it were burned in my brain and eyes.

"I know, Ammy." He rubbed my back with one hand while the other kept me firmly anchored to him. "I wouldn't ask if I didn't think it was important."

I sniffled, accepting the truth in his words. Pushing the details out was like shoving at boulders, each dislodged with great effort. "She came to the house maybe a few months before. She was meant for Junior, and he took her to wife. She wasn't happy, even though he'd put her in the consort's suite. She didn't talk to us, treated the unmarried girls like we were less—or at least she did with most of the other women. She'd talk to me sometimes, when I tidied her rooms, and we were friends." I sagged against him as the words slid out a little easier and sighed. "She came from another place. She told me where, but I don't remember. Said she'd been some kind of princess, but she came to detest Junior and Master. She fell pregnant, and Junior became even more pompous than usual, strutting around saying he was going to be well rewarded for his efforts."

The memory of those days, the constant fear that he'd also notice me, hit hard. "He'd been absent from the house for weeks, then returned, but he was different. That night, she'd been sick and hadn't bent to his will. Refused to attend the affiancing dinner for his younger brother. Eldora had been docile and meeting all his demands, but Junior took it badly. Said it was a loss of face and couldn't be tolerated. She suffered terrible sickness during the pregnancy, not that he worried about it at all."

I sucked in a breath as memories filled my mind.

"He went upstairs, and I heard him shouting at her. The entire household did. She yelled back, and then the screaming started. His and hers. Then silence." I hiccupped and opened my eyes.

"Ammy, what happened?"

Shaking my head was all I was capable of as the tang of bile filled my throat. "He came down a little while later, demanding I assist to clean the suite. There was blood everywhere in the room and on him. I never saw Eldora again. He left that night, returned the next day, but no one said anything. It's the way it was in the sect. She wasn't the first to disappear and likely won't be the last either."

Damien swore, and I felt when his muscles tensed further. "I'm sorry. Sit down and I'll pour you a tea."

He settled me into a chair, then moved away. I scrunched down into the padding of the wooden chair, seeking any warmth I could find. He returned quickly, setting the cup on the table before me and hunkering down. "We'll find her. We'll fix this."

I looked up. "If only you could," I said. No one would ever make this better until the religious groups were disbanded. Andrew and Damien might work together, but I knew there were other cults. They shared connections and women, their reach all-encompassing.

"Damien?"

He glanced at me in silence.

"I want to forget it all. I want to never have to remember any of this."

His eyes closed, but not before I saw the pain in them. When he opened them, he'd erected a wall around the pity. "I know. We'll find out who's responsible, Ammy. They will pay. Junior will pay for killing Eldora. As will Master. But first we have to find out who's following you. Find out why they nearly killed the children and murdered those on Andrew's dirigible. They must be brought to justice."

He was right, but it didn't quell the terror that lived deep inside me.

I could never go back. I'd rather die first.

Chapter Eleven

Francesca sat beside me at the table. This was the third night she'd joined us for dinner, and she was clearly feeling a little more comfortable given the shy way she answered the junior lieutenant's query.

"My brothers and sisters are fun, but downstairs is a little stifling."

The young man in his teens was showing a distinct fondness toward her, and I didn't want to encourage it. Thankfully, the sweets were being rolled in.

We waited in silence as they were placed before us. Then Francesca turned to me. "What is this?"

The icy dessert was unlike anything I'd ever seen before, and I turned to Damien.

"Sorbet," he informed us, and I watched as he raised his spoon and scooped some of the pink concoction up. "Try it," he suggested.

I followed suit and tasted it. "Strawberry!"

The captain laughed. "Yes, Ms Coultihan. We try to ensure anyone travelling with us has at least a varied array of delicacies to try."

"Indeed you do, but when are we likely to make landfall?"

Damien coughed. "The captain has assured me that late tomorrow we should see land. We'll pull into port the morning after, unload the cargo, and I'll plan for the house to be made ready. We should be able to leave the ship in two days."

Not that I didn't like the ship. That wasn't it at all. But I was feeling the effects of being cooped up for so long with nothing to see but the sea.

Francesca smiled. "The boys will appreciate that! They're sick of the cabin and only being able to walk around once a day. They're going to get themselves in trouble soon. Mama always said you couldn't coop up a good boy, let alone one meant for trouble." Then her face dropped. "Is there any news?"

Damien shook his head. "No, I'm sorry, Francesca. Mrs Coultihan had her brought to her house, and we'll hear when the time comes."

The girl's lower lip trembled. "May I be excused please, Sheriff? Captain? Miss Ammy?"

She was grieving and putting a brave face on it. Even though her mother had not yet passed, she clearly felt the loss keenly.

"Of course," I offered with a soft voice. My heart ached for the younger girl.

Francesca left the table, and the door slid shut behind her. The young lieutenant rose to follow her, but Damien shook his head. "I don't think that would be appropriate."

He returned to his seat, and I wordlessly thanked Damien for his help. I knew Francesca was unaware of the lieutenant's interest. She was also not in any condition to accept any advances he might make. Besides, she'd told me she wanted to become a doctor, and unless she changed her mind, I would not allow someone to come between her and what she most desired. She'd gone without so much in her youngest years that I would fight to give her what she wanted.

As the bowls were collected, the captain suggested coffee. I excused myself, surprised to see Damien follow suit. Once in the hallway, I turned to him. "I need to check on Francesca."

He nodded and followed without a word. His presence reassured me, and by the time I'd reached the suite, I felt better. Opening the door, I glanced inside, and there on the sofa sat Francesca. Streaks smeared her cheeks.

"Jessie is in the cabin with the boys," she murmured. "They were restless."

"I'm sorry, Francesca. I can see you're upset."

She shook her head. "I knew she was sick. We kept it from the others for as long as we could, but Simeon realised it before anyone else. Mama always said it would be the death of her, the religion, and I guess it was, in a roundabout way. But Papa is dead, and Mama…"

I wound my arms around her. "I know I can't be your mama. But I can be your friend, Francesca. If you'll let me." I meant it. Every word.

She nodded and dropped her head to my shoulder. I glanced back at Damien, who waited by the door, his face soft with sadness as Francesca cried silently in my arms.

Tears pricked my eyes, but I blinked them away because she needed me to be strong. To be there for her.

Gradually, her grip on me eased, and she tugged away. "I'm sorry, Miss Ammy. I shouldn't have done that."

I mock scowled. "Yes you should. Your mama asked me to care for you. All of you. That's exactly what I plan to do. I understand your fears. I grew up in Haven House."

Her spine stiffened. "You're one—"

Before I could argue or explain, Damien advanced and crouched down. "Miss Ammy isn't. She got away. Escaped, the same as you have. She understands how you feel. Her mama died, and so did her papa. She has her brother, but they don't really know each other."

I almost dissolved into a puddle, because everything he said was right.

I loved Andrew and was grateful he was alive. As for our other siblings, I didn't yet know what had become of them. We'd had so little time together. I'd been alone a long time and had spent so many years controlling myself, my impulses, and being strong for me that I hadn't let my guard down during the few weeks I'd been with him and Gloriana.

His glance caught me by surprise, but in his eyes, I read acceptance and something else.

Francesca pulled away. "I… I'll be all right now. It just crept up on me. Surprised me is all."

I watched sympathetically as she swiped at her eyes. "It'll come back. Creep up on you. When you feel sad, it's okay to ask for help." I kept my words quiet, so no one outside the room heard them.

Her tremulous smile assured me she understood. I just hoped that one day, I could also mourn as she had.

"We'll leave you now," Damien said and took my elbow, steering me from the room.

When the door shut, he spun me slowly. "You believe everything you said, and yet who do you lean on, Ammy?"

I opened my mouth, then closed it again. There was no answer, because who could I possibly rely on?

He pulled me close. The move was gentle, and I sighed. "I wish I'd had someone when I was younger." I curled my fingers into the lapels of his jacket.

"You've got me now, Ammy. I'm here for you."

When he kissed me, I wanted to melt into the embrace. I wound my arms around the back of his neck and gave in to the pleasure that coursed through me.

He moved with a jerk, swinging me up into his arms.

I tugged back from his lips, saw the glint in his eyes, dangerous with desire and hunger.

The same hunger that burned in my belly.

Striding up the hall, we remained silent, as if communing on a soul-deep level.

We went up the stairs, and when he reached my cabin, he stilled. "If I enter, there can be no going back, Ammy." His voice ground against me, and I shivered.

Right here and now, I needed to decide. Could I accept him, this man, into my life? Could I trust him with who I was?

"Ammy?"

I opened my mouth and slid from his grasp. Did it have to be forever? Couldn't I just take a chance? Grasp what he offered and see where it went?

Selfish, my mind said.

Take it, my body screamed as all my nerve endings quivered with desire.

"I can't promise forever, Damien. I don't know what I can…"

He shook his head, his lips flattening. "No. When you're ready—"

Urgency punched into me, and I grabbed for his coat, hauled him close, and sealed his mouth with mine.

We moved, me pulling him closer and Damien following, the handle of my cabin door biting into my spine. I released one hand and reached back to open it.

I pushed inside while he held me upright as the passion rose and threaded around us both.

He kicked the door shut and lifted his head. "Ammy, don't do this unless…" He gulped as I reached for the bodice of my gown.

"I'm in control of my life, Damien. I want you." I stared at him, unblinking and willing him to understand that for all I was terrified, I wanted what he was offering now.

He reached out and stilled my hand. "I'm a lifetime man. You take me now, then be aware this is forever."

It was my turn to gulp. "I'm…" I squeezed my eyes shut, trying to work out how to tell him I didn't expect that from him and that I wasn't ready for that kind of commitment.

Long moments passed, and I opened my eyes, my gaze roaming over his features.

He frowned. "I can't be with you until you're ready, Ammy."

My hands fell away from the buttons, bodice gaping and revealing the chemise I wore beneath it. "I want this, Damien."

He grimaced. "I want it too, but I want you. I feel that what's between us could be more, so I'm not willing to settle for a simple act of pleasure. I want you, Ammy. I want to love you and live with you. But I won't settle for less. I won't let you settle for less either."

He stepped back, away from me, and I bit my lip. In his voice, there was uncertainty.

"I'm not ready to promise forever, Damien. I don't even know me, let alone what I want."

"Then I'll leave you, Ammy." He turned on his heel and opened the door.

I wanted to call him back. I wanted his passion and the heat of him. I wanted…

What I want terrifies me. Because I do want hearts, flowers, and promises of a lifetime.

I gulped once again and started to call him back, but the click of the door told me it was too late, and I was once more alone.

I slept fitfully. Rising in the morning, I washed my face and noted the dark circles beneath my eyes. On my breakfast tray was a white sheet of paper.

Letitia passed last night.
Andrew

Closing my eyes, I absorbed the blow, well aware that I would need to tell Francesca first, then broach it with the boys. Samson and Simeon were old enough to grasp the gravity of the message, but I didn't think the girls would understand given their ages.

I took extra care, smoothing my hair back, but didn't eat as my stomach roiled. On shaking legs, I made my way down to the suite and was surprised to find the young lieutenant loitering in the hallway. Frustration roared inside me, but I tamped it down.

"Lieutenant, what are you doing down here?" I couldn't control the sharpness of my tone, and he blushed a deep and totally unbecoming shade of beetroot.

"Uh, Miss Amaryllis, the captain gave me this for you. I thought..." He looked down and shuffled his feet. "Miss Francesca..." he garbled.

I huffed. "Thank you. Now, about your duties, sailor," I grouched, as I'd seen Damien do before.

"Yes, ma'am." He escaped.

For a moment, I felt a hint of regret, but it melted away as I opened the missive.

. . .

We expect to make landfall later today. It would be best if the children remained inside until we are assured of their safety.
Damien

Now I wanted to scream. Clearly my decision last night had wreaked more damage than I could have suspected if he was now refusing to talk to me.

Hot tears wanted to leak from my eyes, but I fought them back. "No good ever came from feeling sorry for yourself," I murmured, then opened the door and entered the suite.

It was curiously empty. "Francesca?"

Her head peeked around the corner of the door. She was pale yet composed.

I beckoned her closer. "Is Jessie attending to the children?"

She glanced at me, eyes narrowed. "You have news?"

"Tell Jessie we won't be long, then join me." I know she was attempting to read my thoughts, but she quickly removed herself from view, then returned. I grabbed a shawl, and together we left the room.

Wordlessly, we ascended the steps onto the deck. I steered her to the back, where there was no chance of being spied on. "I received news this morning, Francesca. I'm so sorry, but your mother succumbed last night."

I felt the blaze of heat before she broke apart, sobs ripping through her. I wound my arms around her and held her close, absorbing every move and wishing I could fix it for her.

Finally, her wild sobs subsided. "I n-need..." she stuttered.

"I can tell the boys, if you like."

Francesca shook her head. "No, it should be me."

I had half expected she'd say that. Before she could move away, ready to undertake the ghastly task, I stopped her. "Wait. We're expecting to make landfall today. We need to keep the children in the suite, where they're safe."

She turned her blotchy face toward me, lost and looking very young. "Why?"

"Come, sit down a moment. Let me explain." We settled on the small stairs leading up to the top decks. "We don't know who has created this mess. The dirigible you came to us on was blown up. We have some information, but not enough. The house was breached too, not long after we left, and we're hiding. We don't know for sure that no one knows where we are, so we need to hide until assured of safety."

"But they're not after us, are they?"

I shrugged because I honestly didn't know. If they were after me, it made no sense. I was of little value. The boys hidden in the cabin below had more worth than any of us females. Yet I couldn't quite discount anything, given the way Damien and I had been hunted after our arrival, so I shared as much as I knew because she deserved that and so much more. "I don't understand what's happening, Francesca. None of this makes sense to me."

She nodded. "We should suspend classes today." She turned in my direction. "I'll keep them inside today. Let me know when we should prepare for... whatever."

Francesca tugged the shawl closer around her and, with her head drooped, headed within.

Dissatisfaction ate at me as I glanced out at the sea. Blue and wild. Free. What would that be like?

The thud of footsteps caught my attention, and I looked up.

Damien headed toward me. "You've received my notes?"

"Yes. Thank you, Sheriff." Formality would give us distance, I reasoned. Then I'd be able to think clearly. Not be so emotionally involved with him.

He scowled. "Damien. My name is Damien."

I opened my mouth and closed it again. Gave a terse nod.

"Angry with me? I'm sorry I didn't come down to tell you in person. We've received news that I had to deal with." He hunkered down onto the step beside me.

I bit my lip. "Is something wrong?"

"Yes. My manufacturing plant was broken into last night. My men are looking into it."

I reached out and grabbed his hands. "I'm sorry. Is this my fault? Have I somehow brought these disasters with me?"

He cupped my cheek. "No, Ammy. You didn't. You've done

nothing wrong. I just don't see how all these bits fit together yet. What the connections are." He seethed with frustration.

"I wish I could help you."

"You are. The children?"

"Francesca is telling them. She'll keep them in the suite until you tell us what you need."

He nodded and gazed out the back. "I had never seen the sea before I was twenty-three. Never had a hankering. Then one day, I was sent to the coast. Had to investigate the death of a small-town sheriff. Since then, I've loved the water."

"It's calming, isn't it? And yet it's wild and free at the same time."

Damien laughed. "Best description I've heard in a long time."

I turned to him. "What next?"

"I don't know. We make sure it's safe. Get you and the children on shore and settled. Then we dig deep and fast."

It wasn't really enough, but for now, it would do.

Chapter Twelve

I followed Damien down the gangplank, the structure jouncing beneath my feet. "Is this safe?"

"Absolutely."

I didn't feel satisfied until my feet were on the ground once more.

We headed to the small warehouse and entered the dimness. "Mr Forster?" Damien called.

A little grizzled man with white hair and a heavy stoop stepped forward.

"Damien Whitmore. I gave instructions for the house to be ready. Have you made it so?"

The man nodded. "Good to meet you, Mr Whitmore. The house is ready for your family. This must be Mrs Whitmore? I believe you're travelling with another young woman and your family?"

I jerked sharply in the man's direction, but Damien took my hand. "Uh, yes. We've brought the educational items you requested too."

"Excellent. I'll have Maddison arrange the cart for your family, but if you'd like to look it over?" Mr Forster snapped his fingers, and a youngster scurried forward with a large metal key. It was old-fashioned and heavy, the insignia on the end of an intricate *F* embedded with curlicues. "It was my family home, but I have no children to carry on. I've moved into the small house beside the warehouse here. Better to attend to business, and not quite so many stairs.”

His laugh echoed, but no one smiled or laughed.

Damien thanked him for his help and gave directions for the cargo to be unloaded, then ushered me outside.

High on a hill, not a great distance from the wharf, stood a house, sturdy and imposing, and I followed Damien as we walked toward it.

“You didn’t correct him,” I said once we’d made it some distance from the buildings, finally sure no one would hear us.

“No. You’re a single woman, and I’m a single man. Your reputation would be shredded if anyone knew, Ammy.”

“But it doesn’t change the truth. I’m still a spinster, and you’re still a single man. We’ll be staying in a house together. Francesca and the children aren’t considered adequate chaperones, are they? Questions will be asked at some point.” What a nightmare this could become. None of these issues had crossed my mind before.

He spun around, eyes glowing. “You’re quite right, Ammy. There’s only one way forward, if you’re concerned. Marry me and it settles the issue.”

That stopped me. *Marriage. Forever.*

“I...” I floundered. Right now, part of me wanted the promise in his silky words. Another part said he’d regret it eventually and neither of us would have a way out. My gut moved with a lurch.

“Ammy?” He cupped my chin. “Marry me, Ammy. I know you’re not sure. I know you’re frightened, and nothing has been resolved. I’d give you more time, but you’re right. Questions will be asked. This way, you’re protected, and if anything happened, you’d have my name. That’s no small protection.”

I blinked. “But who...?”

He smiled as if he’d won some kind of game.

“There’s a pastor here. He could arrange the ceremony.”

I gripped his hand, knowing I squeezed hard. *Too much. Too fast.* But what other option was there? My name was all that was left to me. That too would be gone if I married him. Life had stripped away everything else and left me ashes. Would this be the same?

“I...” I blinked, blinded for an instant. “Yes. You’re right, of course.”

He tugged me close, and I burrowed in, letting his words fill the empty bits of me. "I'll have the pastor come to the house tonight. We won't wait any longer. Your reputation must remain unsullied."

Moments passed before he pulled away. "We should get to the house, inspect it, and return to the ship. The others will wait for us."

I let him pull me along, allowing my brain to fill with hope and excitement, because focusing on what I feared, that he might use me, hurt me, and rebuff me, was too scary to consider.

The house itself was nice enough. Large airy rooms, the furniture old and dusty, but more than that, it was sturdy.

We chose rooms for the children. Jessie would take a room in the nursery, while Frank and Aloysius would bunk down in the attic's servants' quarters. The main bedroom, a generously sized area, took up a large portion of the front first floor, complete with bathing chamber and dressing rooms. Its sitting area would have been lush some twenty years ago. Now it simply resembled an old room in need of care. I didn't enter the space, and Damien stared at me, a question in his eyes.

"Ammy?"

"Yes, it's fine," I whispered and retreated from the doorway. "The boys will need a schoolroom," I muttered and then fled.

He let me be, and I was thankful for the mercy he showed. I thudded up the stairs to the second floor and stopped, simply allowing myself to breathe. I clapped my hand over my mouth to stifle the sounds of fear, whimpers that reminded me I was choosing to accept this situation.

I'd run away from Haven House, from a fate I had no choice over, and here I was about to step into the same situation. "It's different," I said, the words echoing in the emptiness.

Is it? Really? My brain teased me with that question, and I shoved it aside with great effort.

The rooms up here weren't as spacious or well appointed. One contained suitcases and dressing equipment, while another held boxes of books, plus tables and chairs. In the corner, I spied a box of toys and tugged it forward.

I retreated to the room I'd seen earlier and sank to my knees before an old sea trunk. It opened with a creak, and I saw the lavender bag first.

I pulled it away until I found a gown, yellowed with age, the material velvety soft.

Now I stood, pulling the gown with me. Lush, though in need of a clean, its long sleeves were decorated with fragile lace, the bodice high enough to not offend but intricately layered.

Even as I slid it to the floor, a bag caught my eye. It was bulky, and I carefully untied the strings. Inside were shoes, matching the gown but so delicate. With care, I removed one of my bulky boots and slipped it off with a thud. My foot fit perfectly in the shoe.

The seed of an idea rose.

Tonight.

Not enough time to clean and dry the gown, but I would see if it fit and anything else within.

I turned my attention to another trunk. Dresses filled it to the brim. Light fabrics, sprigged cotton, and I thought of Francesca.

"Yes, once we're settled, I'll bring her up here." Perhaps we'd even find the tools for her to refashion them to suit herself.

The echo of feet on the stairs caught my attention, and I stuffed the ivory gown back into the first trunk. The lid had only just closed when I turned to meet Damien's eyes.

"You've found something?"

"Clothing treasures." I set about dusting myself off.

"We should return to the ship, Ammy." He reached out a hand, and I took it, because I wanted to.

At the bottom of the stairs, I stopped and glanced back up. "Eldora would have loved this house. She said where she came from, there were verandas and wide-open spaces." I shrugged. "Will you have time to arrange the pastor? Or should we wait until tomorrow?"

"I don't want to wait, Ammy. Do you?" His voice was dark with promise, and I shivered.

"No. Not really." Waiting meant time to reconsider. To change my mind. A dangerous prospect. "I want to... tonight." The word emerged, strangled, and he stopped me with a hand on my shoulder.

"If you're not sure—"

"Damien, I'm not sure I'm ever going to be completely ready. But I won't let Haven take anything more from me. My name and reputation are all that's left. They will not set the direction of my life. I've said yes. I gave my word, and I'll stand by that. By you."

The uncertainty on his face hurt, cutting deeply at me, but I needed him to understand.

"I want what I feel, and to be alive. I don't want fear clouding my thinking. I know you're a good man. You'll be honest with me. What I want most of all is to be close to a person. To know that person is committed to me and me alone. With you, I know that's more than just a chance, and I'm willing to control my fear to take it." It didn't stop the quaking or the terror, but it curtailed the wild desire to run away, because I leashed it.

"I will stand by you. I'm not like the men from Haven, Amaryllis." He jutted his jaw forward, as if daring me to disagree.

In that instant, the fear melted, replaced by a curious peace. "And so we wed, tonight." I rose onto my toes and kissed him. "Forgive me my fears. I spent so long there that I don't know how to live in a world like this."

He dropped his forehead against mine. "We'll work through this, Ammy. Together. You and me."

The kiss he planted on my lips was soft, and it curled my toes up.

"We should head back now. Make the arrangements."

His fingers twined around mine, and we walked in silence together.

I stood in the gown I'd found in the chest, it had been hurriedly cleaned by Francesca, Jessie, and myself. My brushed-out hair was twined into an elaborate coil thanks to Jessie and Francesca, and now we gathered in the front room of the pastor's house.

The light of the candles glowed, and the children watched, hushed, as Damien and I made our promises.

Then, taking Constance into my arms, Damien following suit with Faith, and Francesca herding the boys, we headed to the house on the hill.

Lights glowed, welcoming us home.

It wasn't large and overwhelming, like Damien's house or Andrew's.

It didn't terrify me like Haven House. I wondered at the portent of my thoughts.

We'd eaten before the ceremony aboard the ship, so tonight we would simply usher the children up the stairs to their beds before taking some time to ourselves. Jessie, having acted as witness along with Aloysius, now marched them all up the stairs, including Francesca.

The weight of the ring Damien slid onto my finger reminded me that I'd taken a step that couldn't be undone.

We moved to the veranda, and Frank emerged with a tray, glasses of wine and a bottle resting in a cooler.

"We need to let Andrew know," I murmured.

"Tomorrow. We can take time for that then. Tonight is for us."

Frank disappeared back inside, and the intimacy of the two of us, alone in the night air, left me shivering with reaction.

"Your family should have been there, Ammy. I regret that it's not the romantic event most women look forward to."

The gravity of his words, the concern on his brow, had me turning toward him.

"I never dreamed of a wedding, Damien. I'm not sure I know what's normal there. In Haven, the women were bound to the man, a ring placed on the finger, and a dinner, before he took her off and—" I stopped, because the term that rose to mind seemed eminently wrong tonight.

"What?" he urged.

"No. Not tonight, Damien." I stared into the darkness, wondering if I was ready for what came next, though. Intercourse. The word floated through my mind. Knowledge of what it was, what it meant had me biting my lip.

"Ammy? If you're not ready, we don't have to do anything. Not until you're ready."

The oxygen in my lungs escaped with a whoosh. "I don't know what I'm ready for just yet, Damien."

"Then we can wait. Take it at a pace you're ready for."

I drank my wine, letting the bubbles tickle the back of my throat as I considered what he'd said. The offer reinforced the differences between him and the men of Haven.

I finished the wine, set down my glass. "I'm tired."

"Then we shall retire." My husband—how strange that term was—scooped up the tray, and I followed him to the kitchen.

He took my hand, and together we made our way up the staircase to the main bedroom.

"You bathe first. I'll make up the couch."

I shook my head. Just because I wasn't yet ready for any more didn't mean he shouldn't be comfortable. "No, share the bed. I mean, it's large enough."

His gaze burned me, but I refused to turn away like a coward.

"I'm not sure..."

I smiled. "I am. Now, I'll go bathe and change."

On quick feet, I scurried away, nightgown in hand. The lights glowed, and I wondered once more at the change in circumstances. When I re-entered the bedroom, my shawl firmly wound around my shoulders, I headed for the bed, pulling back the covers. "It's a good thing Mr Forster could arrange women to come in and clean so quickly."

Damien grunted, peering over the tiny communicase he held.

"Is something wrong?"

He glanced up. "The damage to my house is worse than I expected. They also tried to interrogate my men."

He slumped down to the bed, and I crawled toward him, placing my hand on his shoulder. "I'm so sorry, Damien. If I hadn't—"

He whirled and grabbed at my shoulders. "No. It's not your fault, Ammy. Don't say that." Damien surged up, away from me, and stalked to the end of the bed. "Go to sleep. I'll bathe and be back shortly."

I felt the loss of him like a cold wave washing over me, and it stung. Here I'd given him a promise, the same as he'd done to me, but when it got tough, he'd left to work through it alone. I realised now that was also how I coped.

"Then we're just going to have to change, aren't we?" I murmured.

Exhaustion clawed at me, and I slumped down, pulling the covers over myself and settling on my side. "Tomorrow."

When I woke, it was to sunshine peering through the windows, the bed covers tossed to the side, and the outline of him on the sheets.

I blinked, because I'd expected him here. Pulling myself from the bed was an effort, given the nip in the air.

Sounds echoed from outside, and I moved to the window to peer out. The children played on the lawn, carefree, rushing around while Francesca perched on the edge of a chair, book in hand. Jessie kept an indulgent eye on the movement.

I turned and headed to the dressing room, eyeing the other gown hanging there. *Not the blue one. Not today*, I told myself and tugged it from the hanger.

With quick movements, I dressed, then tidied up my hair before leaving the bedroom.

I moved down the stairs with quick, jerky movements and went to the front door. I was about to go out when Aloysius appeared before me, stepping from the dark corner.

"Miss Ammy, Master Damien asked me to give this to you."

A folded sheet of paper was thrust at me, and I took it, glanced around, and then went into the parlour. Settling myself on a seat, I began to read.

Ammy,

Forgive my absence, but I've been called back to the ship. Information was received late last night once you were asleep. Information I must deal with immediately.

I don't know when I'll be back.

This must be dealt with now; otherwise, we're all in jeopardy. Keep the children close to home, and I'll explain when I return.

Damien

I glanced at the ship, then back to Aloysius. "What happened?"

The big man shook his head. "Don't know, just that someone came to the house late last night. They left early this morning, and Master

Damien gave me this. There were angry words. I don't know more than that."

He should have woken me. It ran like a refrain through my head. "Did he leave anything else for me?"

"No, Miss Ammy."

I considered the little I knew. "The children are not to leave the yard. Either you or Frank remain with them at all times. That applies to Francesca too."

Now I whirled away, heading for the kitchen. Tea was high on my list of needs at this point.

I puttered around, heating a kettle, finding a cache of the black leaves and a pitcher of milk.

There wasn't much in the way of foodstuffs, and I checked the kitchen, making a mental list of what would be necessary to feed the ten currently housed here. The basics of meat, fish, vegetables, fruits, flour, etc.

I'd just finished when Frank came racing in. "Miss Ammy!"

I turned and noted the pallor on his face.

"What?" I rushed toward him and he grabbed my arm, dragging me through the house to the front door. There on the horizon, I saw something. It was large, black, and looked mean. "What is it, Frank?"

"A war dirigible, Miss Ammy. It's heading this way." The fear in his tone froze me.

"The children. Get them inside, and send Aloysius to me," I barked and then ran to the library. I hunted for pen, ink, and paper, then madly scrawled a note.

D

What do I do now?

A

I'd barely pushed it into Aloysius's hand when a figure came bobbing up the path. I pushed Aloysius forward. "Go," I murmured and watched as the black airship came ever closer.

They've found us.

Would nowhere be safe for us?

"Will we be hunted forever?" I rubbed my hand over my face, feeling the surge of pain from the pressure, and looked away. I wouldn't show anyone my tears of fear. They didn't deserve to know that the terror cut me to my core. Especially if it was someone to do with the mess from Haven House.

One deep breath. Another. I forced my body to relieve the pressure and hoped like hell I was making a good choice.

"Ammy!"

"Damien? *Damien!*" I hurried forward, toward the man who was running toward me. Aloysius found him first, and I was mortally aware of the transport looming ever closer. Terror froze my marrow, and I shivered in response.

Damien caught me up, pulling me close. I wanted to take refuge in his embrace, but the dirigible was getting closer.

"Damien, we have to go!" I started disentangling myself before I registered that he wasn't moving.

"It's okay." He bracketed my face with his hands, forcing me to look at him. "It's another of Andrew's ships."

I kept moving, struggling, until his words arrowed into my brain, burrowing deeper.

"What?" I stopped, suddenly limp. "What do you mean, one of Andrew's ships?"

He held up the communicase. "He has news. Information. Something he couldn't share, so he used his attack dirigible. Gloriana is on board too, bringing clothes and supplies."

The absence of fear left me light-headed. "No danger?"

Damien shook his head, smiled, then hauled me close and kissed me. Hard. In view of everyone. I wound my arms around him, returning it, because it brought with it a sense of life, safety, and security.

When he let me go, my breathing was rapid, but I smiled. Who wouldn't?

A sound filled the air, the rattling hum of an engine, and I looked up, noting the dirigible's proximity.

"Where will it land?"

He pointed to a distant field still near enough to walk. By now, others had come out to gawk at the sight, and I looked at them. The township held several hundred people, including children, who jumped and ran around once the first flush of surprise passed.

Clusters formed, arms reaching as they pointed and chattered like birds, and I watched them. Not too long ago, I had been like this, surprised at the sight of a flying ship.

Damien slid an arm around my shoulder. "We'll go down and meet them."

I nodded absently. "I'd like my shawl, though," I said, and he squeezed my shoulder.

We trudged up the hill I'd run down, the silence between us companionable. I had plenty of questions, but they'd wait until later. These were my first guests, and I'd do right by them.

Jessie emerged as we entered the house, her face pale. "What's happening, Miss Ammy?"

I opened my mouth, but Damien began to explain, so I hurried up the stairs to find my heavy shawl. That nip was turning cold as the wind blew, and I wondered if a storm would hit.

As I reached the bottom of the stairs, Jessie was ushering the children up the staircase, their faces sober, though Francesca was promising to read to them. The littlest two were tiring, eyes drooping over chubby cheeks. I thought of the room upstairs and the trunks. There was plenty of material, and those gowns... surely some could be reworked quickly? I'd already seen the results of Francesca's handiwork in the gown she'd worn the night before to dinner at the captain's table.

"Francesca, tomorrow, I have something special for you. And tonight, you'll join us for dinner with Andrew and Gloriana. The younger ones will eat in the nursery with Jessie."

Her eyes widened, and she nodded. "Yes, Miss Ammy."

I stopped her with my gaze. "Not Miss Ammy. Just Ammy. Promise me?"

Her lips turned up in a small smile. "Yes, Ammy."

I felt like we'd turned an important corner, and perhaps it was the start of a genuine friendship.

Chapter Thirteen

The meal passed with happiness and laughter. Francesca sat beside me, glowing with pleasure at being included among the adults. Andrew had already expressed his dissatisfaction at Damien's and my change of circumstances, though he gave in once we assured him we'd fully considered what we were doing. He could see we were committed to the choices we'd made.

When Frank removed the last of the dishes, Francesca made her departure back upstairs to her room, and the rest of us settled in the office.

"You've news, Andrew?" Damien's voice was dark and tense.

"Yes, but first, Ammy, do you remember where Eldora came from? That's her name, right?"

I glanced at Andrew. "No. I mean, yes, it's her name, but no, I don't remember where she came from. Only that they were stronger and more important. Another sect."

My brother sighed and handed over a piece of paper. "Haven House was attacked last night. Junior, Master, and some of the men disappeared."

My heart thudded heavy and slow. "What do you mean, they've disappeared?"

Andrew grimaced, and I turned to Gloriana. She simply shook her head. "They turned up the day you left, but this time I mean, they were seen running from the building right after a posse of men entered along with human automatons, I believe. They wore uniforms with NC on them."

I blinked. "Automatons? How could they get here?"

Damien gripped my hand tight. "Men as automatons? I thought that level of replacement was outlawed?" The fury in his growl fed the rising panic in my chest.

"They are. The only house we know of with NC is Nobel Crest. But whoever they are—"

I squeaked, looking down at the paper clutched in my hands. Read it, blinked, and read it again. "Nobel Crest. Eldora came from there. Said Nobel was her family name." I glanced up at my brother's face.

"You said you didn't know," he sputtered.

I shook my head. "I said I didn't remember. Different. They're powerful, aren't they?"

Andrew nodded.

Damien released my hand, then rose from his seat and stalked around the room. "So, they attacked Haven House? Why?"

"That we don't know definitively. Gloriana helped some women. She's got other information."

My sister-in-law nodded. "It seems Eldora was sent to Haven. The oldest daughter and the only one unmarried. It was an agreement. Haven House would grow, both in stature and size. Junior would receive certain help, including some replacements. His hand was the first step, it seems. He would, for a period and once the upgrades were completed, become an enforcer for Nobel Crest. Learn about them, their ways, and how to increase Haven's reach." With a shaking hand, Gloriana brushed away a curl that had come free from her hairstyle, her gaze on mine. I read her loathing of the situation, understood it. *Shared* it. "But when they heard no more concerning the birth of the child promised, they became suspicious. Questions were asked, and it seems Ammy was the only one with any definitive information concerning her whereabouts."

Damien spun back to me, his gaze hyper-focused. "Ammy? They're chasing Ammy? She's not involved and knows nothing."

I wanted to dissolve into a puddle on the floor, but that wouldn't help anyone.

"Yes, though they don't know who Ammy is. The enforcers for Haven certainly know she has information, but Nobel Crest only know that someone assisted Junior the night Eldora disappeared. The Nobel Crest men took two of the Haven wives, younger girls who may not know what happened, which may be a godsend." Gloriana's words didn't instil confidence in me.

"We need to find out what the hell Junior and Master are up to. We need to find Eldora, and we need to keep Ammy safe." Damien bit out his summation.

A thought struck me. "So, why are they chasing the children?"

All three gazes landed on me. Gloriana bit her lip, Andrew looked shocked, and Damien's face was full of consideration.

"You have the children. There's a connection to you, so if they can't get to you, they'll chase the children knowing you'll try to save them." Damien spoke slowly, as if working the theory over.

Andrew nodded. "That would make sense."

The fiery burn of bile rose in my throat. "No. We'll send them away. Somewhere safe—"

"Where, Ammy? Because they've got resources and connections, as we now know. We have to find the root of the plot and deal with it." Damien's hands rested on my shoulder, and I sighed and burrowed closer. What else was there to do?

My head ached, my guts twisted, and every turn my brain made just raised more problems and issues. "I—"

Gloriana reached out, took my hand. "We should retire for the evening, my love." She rose, and though I made to do the same, Damien stilled me, and I saw the understanding in her gaze. "We'll see you in the morning. Perhaps some rest will give us perspective."

Damien trailed them from the room as I considered the importance of everything I'd been told. It made little sense right now. How could it? I knew so little, and that made our situation even more dangerous.

I rose and turned to the door, but Damien was back, his eyes shadowed. "I've something else to tell you."

My hand rose to my brow. "Of course." I settled back into the seat and waited for the next blow to fall.

"I received word today about the breach on my home. Our home," he corrected himself. "They tried to gain the information from my staff, as I expected. So far, they haven't uncovered the connection of this home to my businesses, but it's only a matter of time. When they do..." He glanced away. "I needed to send for men. Men who owed me a debt. It will take at least a week for them to arrive, but they'll protect the children and you." He looked to the window.

"Damien? What aren't you telling me?"

"There are strangers prowling the waters between here and Port Isaacs. Looking for a ship. Looking for *our* ship. I have to send it back to where we boarded, but that means we'll be unprotected until my men arrive."

Now I understood his fears. If they worked out where we were, knew we were unprotected, then the danger would be more extreme. "They have power, money, and connections," I surmised.

Damien nodded. "I plan to use the communicase to contact my office tonight. See who—"

Now that was weird. "Why tonight? Not in the morning?"

He laughed. "My men work all twenty-four hours in the day, but it just happens to be that my strategic team are working on a recent development and prefer to do it at night, when there are fewer around."

I rubbed my eyes.

"You're tired," Damien murmured.

"I am, but tell me what else. Then perhaps we should retire?"

"My men will see who they know, what they can find out about the Noble Crest sect."

I nodded. "All right, then. I'll go up and prepare for bed. Join me when you're finished." I rose, nerves twanging. Would he read into the implicit invitation I'd just offered?

Damien frowned. "I won't be long."

I left the room, moving with the loose gait of someone nearing the end of their energy. Each step was an effort. Once I entered the room, I sighed and slumped to the bed before reaching down to remove my ugly shoes. My plan for today, taking Francesca to the attics, had been shelved, but perhaps tomorrow? Then I might go through the assorted items. Find more footwear to replace these I had now worn for well over a week. At least the stink of the night-cart adventure had finally evaporated.

I lay back and gazed at the ceiling. I promised myself I'd close my eyes for just a moment, then head into the bathing room.

Gentle touches roused me from the half dream I'd sunk into. "What...?"

Damien's face loomed close, and for a moment, lost in the soft and dreamy cloud, I reached up and took his face in my hands. "I missed you," I whispered and leaned up, needing the touch of him. The taste on my tongue.

He jerked, then settled into the embrace, his hands moving from my shoulders to my waist.

His heat enveloped me, and I felt an urgent need to do more. To have more.

I pulled back slightly so I could whisper against his lips. "Kiss me back."

His eyes, that dark green, flashed at my demand. "If I do, I may not stop, Ammy."

The whisper of his breath slid over my lips, and I licked them, that dark desire that I'd banked now rising and filling my nerves.

"Please," I whispered.

He leaned close, his mouth surrounding mine, his lips forcing mine apart so his tongue could surge deep. I moaned as his hands moved, roaming over the material, cupping my breasts through the layers.

He levered me back so he half lay on me, the weight glorious as he investigated my body, every move fanning the blaze that started inside me. It pushed my temperature to a soaring point, and I was sure my skin would split and expose the fire I couldn't contain deep inside my body.

He moved, lips gliding along my jaw, nibbling and tasting, and I arched, legs widening to invite him closer.

"Ammy, my sweet Ammy," Damien crooned, his lips now wandering down my throat, and those nerves screamed out for more.

I grabbed his hair with both hands. Between each gasping breath, I panted, "Don't leave me tonight, Damien. I want you."

His gaze pierced me. "Do you know what you're asking, Ammy?" He wasn't unaffected if the rapid rise and fall of his chest was an indicator.

"Yes," I answered. *Congress.* I knew the ins and outs of the act. During my time at Haven, I'd seen it more than once, but never had I wanted to participate. With Damien, everything changed.

He tugged me up, his hands moving to his shirt, but I stilled him. "No, I..." Finishing what needed to be said was impossible. My mouth felt woolly and thick, or perhaps it was because I'd never said the words before. Never acknowledged that I could feel this pressure between my legs or the wanting in my breast.

"You want to help me?" I couldn't miss the teasing tone.

The pressure inside me evaporated a little. My hands shook as I reached for him and found the first button. It was tight, and I fought to undo it. Then another. Each one easier than the last until my hand rested just above the buckle of his belt. The evidence of his passion was very much on display, and I gulped. "How...?" I waved an ineffectual hand at the metal, and he laughed.

"Watch. I'll do it this time."

I may have blushed a furious red, but I would not miss this lesson. Not if it allowed me access to Damien and the relief that I was sure lay on the other side of this activity.

He tugged the belt, loosened the tongue, and I watched, committing the movements to memory. With a deft pull, the belt flew across the room, and I was already reaching to pop his pants free.

"Maybe you should slow down a little?"

I stopped and considered. "Why?"

He laughed. "So I can return the favour."

"Please do, kind sir."

He reached out and found the buttons of my bodice. It was a plain and unadorned black wool, and I watched his hands work carefully, releasing one button, then another. When it gaped open, his face flushed, eyes sparkled, and lips curved into a satisfied smile.

In the lamp's glow, the muslin of my blouse appeared nearly translucent. I didn't cross myself, though, because I was closer to heaven now than at any other time. I shrugged off the upper section of my gown in silence, watching him.

My hand moved to the tiny closure at the side of my skirt, and my finger caught on a hook. It hurt.

"Not a dream," I whispered, and suddenly I knew none of this was make-believe. I was here with Damien, ready to pounce on him like a jaguar intent on its prey.

The heat flashed to frigid before reverting to scorching embarrassment. "Oh, Damien, I'm sorry. I thought..." Owning up to what I thought this was would be horrific, but I needed to make him aware that I was no doxy. I clasped my cheeks. "You must think me terribly fast." The words emerged as a mumble.

He turned beet red. "I... I apologise," he muttered and reached for his pants and belt.

"Damien... I meant—"

"No, Ammy. It's my fault. I thought you wanted—"

"I do!" I wailed, and he stopped. Narrowing his gaze on me, he then slumped with a sigh to the bed beside me.

"Tell me what you want, Ammy. I'm a mere simple man and clearly didn't read your intentions correctly."

I gulped, aware I'd made a hell of a mess of this. I covered my eyes with a hand. "I want you, Damien. But I thought this was a dream, so I let it keep going without considering how wanton I must appear."

His frown made me feel even worse. "You want me but thought it was a dream. You felt you could act like this because it was a dream, but when you realised it wasn't, you stopped because you were embarrassed?"

"Yes. Except I really..." The words couldn't push past the lump in my throat.

"You shouldn't ever be embarrassed by this, Ammy. We're married. It's allowed and, in some cultures, expected."

My eyes fluttered against my hand. He pulled it away, so I looked at him. In the depths of his eyes, I saw emotions I was too afraid to name.

"But it's not seemly."

"Why?"

I wet my lips. "Women are submissive. That's their role. To carry and care for—"

He reared back. "That's the sect talking, Amaryllis. Wanting is normal. Passion is not just acceptable but desirable in a relationship like ours. Don't be confused by the rubbish put into your head in Haven House. Do you think Andrew and Gloriana don't have a relationship of love that includes passion?"

My breath hitched. I'd seen them together during the weeks I'd stayed with my brother and his wife. The times I caught sight of them around the corners or in the garden, the brief but highly charged embraces. "I... No, I mean, yes."

"Amaryllis. You're not a child. You've taken the first step to becoming yourself in this place. If you want me, and you want the intimacy, all you have to do is ask. I won't push for what you're unready for, but be aware that I want you. I want the hot, naked woman inside that ugly dress. I want the tenacious woman who freed herself from the situation she'd had to accept."

He cupped my cheek. "But most of all, I desire you, because you fill me up. You tempt me and woke the man who never thought he'd find a love like this."

Those words stopped me. "Love?"

He sighed. "Yes, Ammy. The first time I saw you in that ugly, torn gown with Gloriana, I was hit by a bolt of lightning. Later, I used every opportunity—and trust me, if Andrew didn't see how thin some of them were, then he's not the man I thought he was—to be around you."

My hands clenched. "So, if I want something, I should just... ask?" I held the oxygen in my lungs as his eyes roamed my face. He nodded in answer. "Damien? Will you love me?"

The planes of his face settled into granite hardness. "Now?"

I nodded, then reached for the fastener of my skirt and released it. It fell to the floor, leaving me in my underthings before him. There may be more layers to divest, but this was like being naked before God. Nothing to protect me now.

"Would you like me to remove my pants or shirt?"

Oh Lord! I wanted to say both but stammered out, "Sh–shir–t."

He smiled, and it filled me once more with heat as his eyes promised darkly exotic things.

He divested himself of the white material, revealing his chest, a light sprinkling of chest hair, and my fingers itched to play in it. To twine it and tug him closer.

As if he read my mind, he smiled. "Touch me, Ammy."

I reached out and found the flat disc of one nipple. It budded, and I felt the thud of his heart beneath the warm satiny skin.

"More," I whispered and noted the way the musculature of his belly tightened as I breathed on him.

"Yes," he muttered and reached for his waistband, then stopped. "You do it. You know how."

I employed both hands, tugging at the buttons and releasing him. The material pooled at his ankles. He stepped back, kicking the offending trousers out of sight, and I focused on his white underdrawers, the way they pouched at the front to cover his erection.

His hands settled on my shoulders, then slid down. He lifted me from the bed and turned me, and I felt him undoing the ribbons of my camisole, then brushing it away. His hands settled in my hair and slowly removed the pins holding it up so it fell down.

"You have beautiful hair, Ammy. Like a silken cloud," he murmured, the heat of his breath bathing the back of my neck. I shivered, feeling my body respond, nipples turning to hard buds and rasping against the chemise below my corset.

He turned his attention to the strings of my stays, and I knew I couldn't turn back. My body was on fire with need.

"Damien?"

I turned as he threw the material and boning to the chair near the bed.

Curling my hands over the hot sinewy flesh of his shoulders, I leaned in, as did he. When our mouths met, it was a soft caress, his lips roaming over mine, drugging me. The sensation of his fingers sliding their way over the last scrap of fabric between our skin was arousing.

I closed my eyes, unable to cope with the overload of sensations, the fizzing in my veins, the heat and scent of him, his taste.

With almost nerveless fingers, I gripped his hips, my hand contracting around the tie at his waist.

"Free me, Ammy," he whispered against my ear, and I moved blindly now as his mouth once more found skin. The tie gave as I tugged it, and he hissed in concert with the whoosh of fabric.

Then I was moving, falling, and resting on the counterpane of the bed, his fingers burrowing beneath the chemise and pushing it up so he could slide his fingers over my breasts. The tips were beads of pure pleasure, and when his finger slid over them, I bucked and called out.

Reality melted away. He released the petticoat and pushed it down along with the pantalets I wore beneath it, and then we were skin against skin. The heat of him scorched me as I writhed. His mouth found the tender peak of my breast, sucked it into his mouth, and his tongue danced wickedly against the flesh.

A hand slid down my front, finding the curls that hid my most secret recesses, combing through before sliding between the flesh, now damp and slick with the moisture of my arousal.

"Ammy," he groaned. "I want you."

"Please," I begged, head thrashing in time with the wild thrumming inside me. The urgency built, pressure in my belly hot and raging.

Empty, so empty. I pulled him close, my hands digging into his shoulders as my legs found their way around his waist, my body demanding fulfilment.

Then he was there, nudging against me, and the heat and hunger pushed me on. Lips mating, hands questing, and the sounds of moans and entreaties echoing.

We moved at some point, though I didn't know how. Now I was on the bed, and he was crawling over me, shaking and slick with sweat.

"Now, Damien," I demanded, and as his mouth settled once more over mine, he pushed, shoved. I felt him. Then came the burning sting, and I cried out, startled, and held myself still.

"Stay still, my love," Damien whispered, holding me close. "It'll pass soon."

But I'd squeezed my eyes together to banish the burn and pushed at him. "No. It hurts," I whimpered.

He dotted kisses on my forehead as time segued from one moment to the next in a blur of discomfort.

"Please," I whispered again, and he moved. "Not like..."

The burn wasn't totally gone, though it was receding. Now I felt something more. He shifted his hips, only a nudge, but while my expectation was of fiery pain, it didn't happen.

"It won't ever be like that again, my Ammy. Trust me." He shook, sweat rolling off him, but it didn't repulse me.

The next nudge had me sighing as the passion that had washed away returned by degrees. The next move had me groaning. "Oh, Damien!"

Our lips met and clung, and now his length slid deeper. I felt it, every inch, as I stretched to accommodate him.

"My beautiful wife," he crooned. "Mine. My love."

I joined him now in the dance, our bodies sliding together in an ancient duet that grew faster. Wilder. Hotter.

"More," I demanded of him. And he gave me everything, hands sliding over my skin, urging me to find the precipice. I did. That shining instant where I could no longer hold on to reality.

Splintering.

Burning.

I broke apart, the orgasm unexpected and overwhelming, but I welcomed it because the pleasure filling me was so all-encompassing. I cried out, and his fingers dug deep, the movements of his body urgent and driving while every inch of civilisation cracked and flew away.

The bed groaned, he growled, and I strangely felt truly complete. As if this act of congress had sealed the promises we'd made.

It was as if my heart was whole.

He held me close, and I felt a sensation of jetting deep inside me. I knew what was happening.

I wanted it and the result that may come from our lovemaking. If I were pregnant from this, I would welcome and love the child. Not just because of the teachings of Haven House but because if I were, the child was started by our choice, not the decisions of some self-ordained priest. The teachings of Haven House might dog me for the rest of my life, but I would glory in the fact that I'd chosen for myself.

When Damien finally slumped against me, I held him close, my hands making slippery circles on his flesh.

And finally, the world swam away as sleep overwhelmed me.

Waking was slow, layers of awareness making themselves known. Warmth, an ache, and an unfamiliar languor. I turned, or attempted to, and met something warm and... *naked*.

I started up, the cool air sliding over bare flesh. "What?"

A hand reached out. "It's all right, Ammy." A male and sleep-thickened voice I knew captured my attention.

Understanding flooded my mind, and I blinked once. Then again. "Damien?"

"Yes, Ammy?"

"I'm..." I swallowed. "Where are my bedclothes?"

He turned, and I caught sight of miles of flesh, bare and really so very tempting. "This is normal, Ammy. Married couples sleep together. Naked. We're married and—"

"But what about bedclothes?" I croaked.

"Well, we can put them on if you like, but I'd rather not." His hand slid up to my shoulder, and the wanting rose again, heat pooling in my belly.

I tugged the sheets and wound them around me, and he smiled but said nothing. That he was *watching* me was enough to increase my discomfort several times over.

"I should get dressed." With the sheet tight around me, I dashed to the bathing room, hoping I'd be able to overcome my embarrassment before I saw him again.

I looked in the mirror, cheeks flushed a deep red wine and eyes shining while my hair lay mussed around my shoulders. I caught sight of him behind me in the reflection. Looking down, I noted his nakedness, and my gaze flashed up again.

He stepped closer to me. I felt the heat of him burning my suddenly chilled flesh. "There's nothing to be embarrassed about, Ammy." I watched with fascination as he bent down and kissed the bare skin of my shoulder. A frisson of sensation raced through me.

"It's daytime," I groaned as his lips travelled up the length of my throat and settled at the sensitive juncture of my head and neck.

"There's no rule that says we can't make love in the daytime, Ammy. No rules at all. We can make our own."

I shook from the vibrations of his voice, but it was when I felt the tip of his tongue as it flicked at my jaw that I had to fight my eyelids from drooping.

"Oh, Damien," I murmured and released my grip on the sheet.

"Look in the mirror, Ammy."

My eyes fluttered open, and there in the full-length mirror I saw us both. His bronzed skin against my pale milky flesh, green eyes blazing while his hands covered my breasts, plumping them under his attention. They weren't big, but the tips were a rosy hue, the nipples puckered, and I felt the imaginary wisps of eroticism curling around me.

One of his hands made its way down my belly and covered the mound hidden in a thatch of hair. "So beautiful," he whispered. A finger slid between the fleshy folds, and I leaned back into his embrace.

Lost in the haze, I nearly missed the sound of thudding. Could it be the beat of my heart? Except it wasn't, and I tugged away, startled.

Who? Does someone know what we're doing?

Damien cursed, though his gaze held mine for several seconds before he wrenched a dressing gown from the door and marched away, leaving me with a trembling mass of roiling sensations.

I hurried through my ablutions and dressed. Finally presentable, I went to the bedroom to find him jerking on boots. "What's going on?"

He glanced at me, face set in thunderous granite. "Andrew has received news. We need to meet with him downstairs."

I let Damien take my hand and draw me out of the room and downstairs. In the parlour waited food and Andrew. Gloriana had taken up position in one of the armchairs. They rose as we entered the room, and for a moment, I fancied that Gloriana knew what we'd been doing when interrupted. I burned and squirmed internally, then allowed the sensation to wash away. Damien wouldn't tell. That wasn't the man he was.

"Tea?" I queried. Eyes fastened on me, but I kept up the pretence of nonchalance. For Andrew to be here early in the morning, demanding Damien's attention, it had to be of grave import.

Once everyone had a drink and was settled, Andrew cleared his throat. "I believe they know where you are. But I've intelligence about why they want Ammy."

"More about Eldora?" Damien asked, but Andrew shook his head.

"Not exactly. We know they detained some women from Haven. They've been found beaten but very much alive. They were returned to Haven late last night. They, of course, said Ammy would know, as she assisted Junior. They also said they believed she was Junior's lover." Andrew spat the words, and the distaste turned my stomach.

"I'd never—" Before I could finish, Damien was there, hand on my shoulder.

"She was never his, Andrew. Anyone who says that will have to face me."

Strange, really, that his defence, both honest and heated, bolstered me, but I also felt ill at ease hearing the implication. "Never would I stoop to that. I will face these women and vindicate myself."

Damien added nothing, just kept his hand on me, showing solidarity.

"I know. But the men from Nobel want to see you. They're hunting. They've already sent out ships," Andrew explained.

"They're between here and Port Isaacs," Damien added, and my brother gaped at him.

"You knew?"

"I received word last night. It won't take them long to work out where we are. Sending Ammy off isn't the answer. They'll just keep chasing her. So, we'll set the ground rules. They come here, but we make plans of our own. We find out what they know, share what's in our best interests."

Letting Damien speak on my behalf wasn't easy, but watching Andrew's ire rise was unpalatable too. "I'm not sure about that. The safety of the children—" I looked around the room, hunting for the way to explain my fears.

"I understand, Ammy. You fear for the children, but as far as the Nobel Crest followers are concerned, they're simply collateral damage."

I grunted at that. "They shouldn't be. They've just become orphans. They deserve much better than that."

Gloriana rose and wandered to the window. "So, how do we go forward? There are questions. Many questions and few answers. But the danger is increasing, and we're not going forward."

Not true, of course. "Damien is right. It won't take them long to work out I'm here. We need to meet them as equals. Bring their leader here. Share what we know, or at least enough to keep them busy looking for Junior. And speaking of him, has anyone found him yet?"

Andrew shook his head. "That would certainly improve our chances. But no, my men haven't found him yet."

"I have my men chasing some leads, but I haven't had the opportunity to see what they've found out," Damien said from behind me. I ducked my head a little, knowing full well why he hadn't yet checked his communicase.

"Ammy?" Gloriana asked. "Is something wrong?"

Oh dear Lord! "Uh, no. I'm just considering how we make contact." To myself, my voice sounded strangled, and from the way Damien's fingers settled on my shoulder, I knew he understood my reticence too.

"You look—"

"Perhaps Andrew might wish to join me in the library," Damien cut across Gloriana's words.

Grateful didn't explain my emotions right now, because I would not discuss our intimate encounters with anyone. Instead, I drained my cup and invited Gloriana upstairs to find Francesca and share the bounty I'd found.

We found her in the makeshift schoolroom, and while she seemed engrossed in reading to the two youngest girls, she followed us up to the attic space at my request. I opened the door to the tiny room, and we entered single file.

"Is there something you need me to do, Ammy?" Francesca asked.

"Not exactly. I found these trunks." I led Francesca and Gloriana over to the pile hidden behind old dusty furnishings. "Mr Forster sold the house, complete with everything here, to Damien's business. So the day we came to investigate, I found the most beautiful clothing." I opened the first lid.

Francesca's eyes settled on the cotton gown with the pretty lilac flowers and the lacy detail on top. "May I?" she whispered.

"Yes, of course," I answered.

She lifted the gown and beamed. "It's so pretty."

"I saw it and thought of you. I don't know if they'll fit, but anything you think you can remake is there for you."

Francesca stilled, then whirled around. "For me?" she squeaked.

"Yes. But that's not all. Come look at this." I stepped to the other trunk and cracked the lid. The shoes in their bag sat on top of the gown. "What do you think?"

Gloriana gave an "Ahhh" of appreciation while Francesca reached out and took hold of the material. "It's beautiful," she whispered. "I'm sure with a little work it might fit you perfectly, and the colour with a little embellishment..."

"I agree," Gloriana said, and I smiled. This was what I'd hoped for. That she'd see an opportunity and it might help cement a friendship between us, more of a sisterly kind of understanding.

"Would you like to try?" I asked, and Francesca's gaze shot to mine. "You mean it?"

I laughed. "Yes. I never say what I don't mean."

"Oh, Ammy, I don't think I'm good enough. I mean, this fabric is so pretty. I don't want to ruin it." Francesca dropped the material away as she backed up.

I heard heavy footsteps and turned on a sigh. Frank filled the doorway. "Master Damien is looking for you, Miss Ammy. Mrs Coultihan might best come too, I think."

I bit my lip, because the look on his face didn't bode particularly well.

"Frank, would you carry both these trunks down to the sitting room for Francesca?" Without giving either of them a chance to remonstrate, I hurried from the room and down the steps.

Damien clearly needed my help in a hurry, and I would not allow myself to create fears of the unknown. Not here and not now.

I opened the door to the office, and the look on his face had my stomach plummeting. "What's wrong?"

"The ship just radioed. They were boarded this morning by a Nobel Crest ship's crew. They know where we are now and are on their way."

<h1 style="text-align:center">Chapter Fourteen</h1>

Thank heavens Gloriana and Andrew had packed a range of clothes for me. I had no intention of meeting the head of the Nobel Crest sect in either of the two gowns I'd been wearing for over a week.

The green gown fit perfectly, the high neckline reinforcing my deportment. I had a tendency to slump, from all the years at Haven House when I'd hidden from Junior. The forthcoming interview would no doubt test my endurance, but there was no way I'd let them see just how terrified I was.

The gloves on my hands—kidskin, according to Gloriana—hid the chapped quality of my skin, and my hair was immaculately dressed. I might look like some kind of heiress, but underneath it all remained a woman who feared what was to come.

I sat in the parlour's armchair, moments passing to the cadence of the ticking clock.

In the days since Damien's ship had contacted him, everyone had moved with speed. Gloriana had opted to stay behind, much to Andrew's concern. He had launched the dirigible at dusk that very evening to bring back his own personal security squad, including a phalanx of automative dogs. His arrival last evening had calmed

Damien's manic actions, who'd gathered the men employed by him to set up a makeshift security system around the house.

"But these wooden fences won't keep out anyone who's had replacements fitted," I said, inspecting the high walls that had been hastily erected.

Lines I hadn't noticed before had appeared on my husband's face. I wanted to soothe them, but he simply looked to the wharf and scowled. "I have to do something."

The concern that radiated from him spilled out and washed over me. "Andrew will be back." Not that I felt my answer was reassuring. After all, who knew how long it might take to collect the men and return?

Each night we'd finally lain down to rest late, and each morning we rose early. During the day, he'd worked with the men, hammering and sawing alongside them. I worked to ensure the women of the town had adequate resources to feed their men and assist with those who'd suffered accidents in the erection of the barriers. Thankfully, they were neither numerous nor life-threatening. Exhaustion in these last three days had become a faithful friend, if not an ally. "When do you expect them to make landfall?"

He shrugged. "The ship has one of those new cog-driven steam engines. It's faster than most of the fleet. We looked at more of them. Found having more than would would be too impractical for our use," he added absently.

"But?" I prompted.

"It depends. They'd need to travel back to home base, so who knows?"

I glanced over his shoulder. "Something's coming in, Damien." My voice held a strangled quality.

He pulled a small lens-glass from his pocket and peered into the distance where the craft had appeared. He dropped the lens. "It's Andrew," he said in response, and I released the pent-up oxygen from my lungs.

Now, with the night drawing in, I could only hope that the Nobel Crest contingent would take place once we'd had sufficient time to prepare ourselves.

"I'll let Gloriana know. Then we can set about preparing a meal." I pushed out of the chair.

"That sounds like a workable plan." He turned to me, his face hard. "Ammy, we can formulate our plan tonight, but we need to talk."

"Of course," I offered and then backed away, because those words usually boded ill. Whatever it was, though, it wasn't important enough to keep him there right now to share what lay heavily on his mind. Instead, he was striding off, leaving the house, and going into the night, heading to the field where the dirigible had previously landed, while I stood there alone inside the room, having watched him leave.

I gave instructions, then returned to the parlour, where I'd been told to wait by both Damien and Andrew. Should Nobel Crest arrive this evening, we had to present the pretence of being at ease. It sat poorly on me, as if my skin itched to break free from the charade.

Waiting. Patience. Never my strong suit.

A commotion sounded at the front of the house, and I gripped the arms of the chair.

"They're coming," a voice called. It was young and unknown to me. I held those arms tighter as fear flashed hot and sharp inside me.

I'd learned a good many things during my time at Haven House. Cults didn't respect women, seeing them as a commodity to get what they wanted. Finding ways to upset their equilibrium was a double-edged sword, and power was the ultimate outcome.

The plan we'd formulated was to unsettle them, to draw as much information as possible, and to use them far more efficiently than they could use us.

A tray of tea was delivered to the table beside me, and as agreed when Andrew, Damien, Gloriana, and I planned the encounter, I poured a cup for myself. Then the doors shut behind Gloriana as she scurried back out.

Deep, measured breaths fought the rapid cadence of my heart until it slowed.

A commotion rose outside, which told me the men—a guess on my part, but my assuredness came from experience—were coming ever closer. It wouldn't take long for them to walk that distance once they'd made landfall. Moments ticked by.

An itch started between my shoulder blades, but I ignored it. It was only a physical manifestation of my stress.

Footsteps echoed, coming nearer, and then suddenly stilled outside the door. I took a second to squirm, finding a comfortable position. A knock echoed.

This is it.

"Come," I called, and the doors opened. Andrew and Damien flanked a team of three men. Two of them were large, hulking, with impassive faces. The third was older, gnarled, with bright blue eyes. The same as Eldora, I realised.

I raised my hand and beckoned. The five men entered the room, Damien and Andrew shutting the doors behind them.

"Please, be seated," I encouraged the older man. The two bodyguards, for I knew that was what they were, melted back against the walls of the room. This was something I'd seen many times before at Haven House, but it was the first time I'd been an active participant in such discussions.

The older man blinked but took the seat I indicated. Andrew remained by the door, but Damien advanced, moved behind my seat, and laid a hand on my shoulder. It was a display of strength and solidarity.

Tension zoomed through the air. I waited while the man opposite stared at me. On a sigh, he leaned forward. "You're the one known as Amaryllis?"

"Yes." Damien, Gloriana, Andrew, and I had all agreed I'd answer with brief comments in order to keep the balance of power in our favour. I would do my best to uphold that agreement, but a tremor settled under my skin.

"You ran."

I cocked my head to the side and examined the man. "Some might say that."

His brow wrinkled. "You know what happened to my daughter. I demand you tell me." He balled his fists in his lap, but a single bead of sweat settled on his upper lip.

"I don't know. Not really." My gut clenched. Brinkmanship was not a game I had experience of.

His lip curled. "You were seen with him. The son of Haven's Master. You're his whore."

I flinched inwardly, and Damien's fingers dug deep, the insult calculated to upset the subtle balance. I recentred with some difficulty, and a long moment passed.

"I am no one's whore. I was a child bought by Haven to be used as a servant. Like your daughter, who was sold to the highest bidder. By you."

The blue in his eyes turned icy. "I did not sell her. It was an alliance." He rose, body quivering with poorly controlled fury. "You murdered her."

His men stepped forward, and I raised a hand. "I did not." Somehow, I had to defuse the situation. "She was my friend."

That stilled the older man. "Friend?"

"Please sit, take tea with me while we talk."

I waited as he considered, the furious ruby of his features settling to a deep blush. He wasn't as controlled as he wished to be, and I'd need to step carefully here.

"Eldora was the oldest. The one who showed such potential. I loved my daughter."

As I looked at this man, I saw he spoke the truth, at least as he knew it. But nothing could condone the fact that he'd sold her to Junior. He might call it an alliance, but I knew better. I knew the man who'd taken her to wife and killed her.

The fury in the room subsided slightly as I poured him tea, then offered preferences of sugar, milk, and lemon. He refused all but raised the cup as I did with mine. A sip warmed my insides, which were chilling as the discussion wore on.

"Why do you speak and not them?" he asked me, glancing at Damien with interest.

"Because my husband sees me as his equal." I kept eye contact with the man opposite. I wouldn't let him drive the conversation and shelve me. That would change the dynamics, and what we needed to achieve wouldn't happen if I wasn't wary.

Now the man's eyes narrowed. "Your husband?"

I nodded. "I escaped Haven and chose Damien as my husband. You took that option from your daughter."

He sneered, "Women don't know what they want. They must be guided and sheltered."

I laughed at his words, unable to contain the bitterness that crept up my throat. "We are not pets! You do not 'keep' us and give us away as you please." Sickened and furious, I set my cup down, needing a moment to recompose myself. To find the centre so I could continue with this strange interview.

"You have a spine. He must be lucky to have you." I raised my head to spear him with a fiery glance, but before me sat a man who appeared broken. "Eldora was very much like you. She's dead. I know it. He killed her and the child she carried. My grandchild. The one who would inherit it all."

"So why did you send her there?" Damien asked.

The man, still yet unnamed, raised his head. "I'm old. I sired three sons with the first of my three wives, but I wanted to ensure the safety of those coming after me. I made the promise to the Master of Haven while she was in her childhood. I believed Haven was strong and honest. I was assured Travis Haven showed great promise as a leader. My daughter desired a husband of handsome face and strength. I allowed her to make the final decision. She chose him."

I heard the regret in his words and thawed a little. "Junior might be handsome, but he had none of the other qualities you listed. Why on earth—"

"I didn't know why she felt he was right. I didn't question it. His father sent an emissary, gifts, and images. He promised me great things, including you."

Now I reared back, surprised. "Me?" The word came out like a startled squeak.

"Amaryllis?" Damien demanded.

"As a fourth and final wife. Promised me she was untouched. Pure. As soon as she came of age, she would be sent to Nobel to sit at my side. They spun a story. I was weak, hungry to prepare for the last stretch in my life, so I accepted. Eldora was ecstatic, for she truly wanted children and a home of her own."

I blinked. "What do they call you?" Suddenly I had to know, needed to have a name for this man.

"Father."

The moniker made so much sense, but I refused to call him that. I'd had a father, one who'd made a mistake and tried hard to correct it and reclaim me. It was a mistake I'd paid dearly for, but he was my father, and he'd always loved me. That knowledge went bone deep thanks to Andrew's recently explained stories of his remorse.

"What is the name your mother gifted you?" I pushed.

"Adam."

"Adam Nobel?" I needed to know so I could address him, give him the answers, and demand our freedom and safety. Without knowing his name, it weakened our grasp on any kind of understanding and certainly wouldn't stand up to scrutiny. Who would trust an agreement made when you didn't even know your partner's name? "I will tell you all I know, but in payment, I demand you stop chasing us. You do not harass or harm the children under my guardianship."

He blinked. "That isn't me. Junior and Master have both run away with the army they were growing. They're the ones who seek you."

My brow furrowed. "Why?"

"Because you escaped. Because you have aligned yourself with those who are stronger, have what they desire most. Power."

Damien released me and strode forward so he stood beside me. "What would it take for you to join forces with us?"

Nobel glared at Damien. "My daughter. Her remains and justice."

Damien reached into his pocket and drew out his badge of justice, throwing it onto the small table. Nobel picked it up, gaze searching Damien's face. "Enforcement?"

The nod Damien gave him was curt.

"It means nothing. We have agreements with those in enforcement circles." Adam's voice took on a dismissive tone.

"Not my kind," Damien ground out like glass beneath a boot.

Nobel's eyes flashed. "True. Not like you." He drained his cup. "You mentioned children?"

"Five. Orphans who Amaryllis has taken responsibility for parenting. Outcasts from Haven." Damien's voice turned silky, as if daring the man to threaten them.

Nobel frowned. "Outcasts? Children are gifts to be treasured." I heard a thread of surprise in his words. Damien must have too, as some of the tension ebbed from his frame.

"Haven is not some place where the sun always shines. It's not a home where everyone is equal. Servitude, ownership, and retribution reign freely. These children have lost everything, and I'm what stands between them and oblivion." Perhaps I was being overly emotive in my choice of language, but I was left with no other alternative. I would protect the children, even if it cost me my life and freedom.

"Tell me what happened. I will listen and—"

"Will you pledge to protect them, should the time come? That your sect—"

"Family," Nobel corrected me.

I started but composed myself quickly. "That your *family* will protect them should the need arise? In return, we will find your daughter and return her to you."

Nobel stood, his gnarled frame straight. He spat in his hand and proffered it. Revolted, I nonetheless followed suit, spitting in my palm and holding out my hand. We shook.

"I will," he growled.

I settled back in my seat. "The night Eldora disappeared—because that's how it seemed—there'd been a dinner. Junior's younger brother, Alec, was affianced to his first bride, and there was a celebration. The night was important to both Master and Junior, but Eldora had suffered long bouts of illness with her pregnancy. She was showing and was ill that night. I'd delivered her tea and toast when no one else knew. Junior would have refused her that, but she was my friend." I shrugged. I needed him to understand that Eldora had done nothing wrong.

"The other girls thought her haughty, and she was dismissive of them, though I believe she was simply wary. It took time. We talked as I cleaned her suite, and we became friendly. Junior had just returned from several days away, and he was bombastic, full of his self-importance. Crueller than he'd been before, though, and he demanded her attendance at the meal. She refused."

I rubbed my brow, trying to squeeze everything from the memory, give him what he needed for the safety of the five children sheltering upstairs.

"After the meal, he went up there, to the consort's suite, which was hers. They fought. It was loud. Then she screamed." My guts curled and quivered with remembered terror, those sounds shredding my nerves again as I reheard the shrieks. I looked at Nobel. "Then there was silence."

He paled.

"Junior found me, demanded I clean immediately. It wasn't straight after. Some time had passed, but there was blood. So much. It covered the floors, the bed, and even the ceiling. I scrubbed until my hands bled. The bedding was incinerated. Junior left soon after. When he returned the next morning, it was like nothing had occurred. He had her things sent to the attics and took a new wife. He moved her into the consort's suite next to Master's, and no one questioned it. That's how it was in Haven House."

Hot tears burned my cheeks, but I watched the man opposite me. His bottom lip quivered. "I give my word. Find my daughter, and you will have my support and friendship." Nobel stood. "I will return to my ship but will contact you in the morning."

He turned and left the room, his guards following, but I was frozen in place. The horror of what I'd seen, heard, and been forced to do was unwilling to be banished.

Damien squatted beside me. "You did what you had to do to survive, Ammy."

I nodded. "Yes."

He sighed. "You should come and eat."

The thought of food soured my stomach. "No. I wish to bathe and go to bed." I was exhausted. Emotionally wrung out, and with nothing more to give, I rose. "Goodnight."

Chapter Fifteen

I heard the door open, knew Damien came to me, but I lay still, gaze on the open window, welcoming the breeze because it dried the tears on my cheeks.

"I know you're awake." The bed moved beneath me as he settled behind me.

"I couldn't face food or anyone, Damien. It was horrible, and remembering... Each time, I see and hear more. The scents and sounds."

He gently touched my shoulder. "I can't share that burden with you, much as I'd take it on, Ammy."

I turned. "Eldora and the others were pawns. Just like I was. Dispensable and disposable."

"Yes."

"We have to find Junior and Master. Make them pay for their sins. Find Eldora, or her remains, and send them back." My mind whirled. "We have to go back to Haven."

"Yes."

"The children..." I didn't want to take them back. There was nothing but terrible memories and hardship there for them. Nothing for me either. I'd pledged myself to Damien, and his home was not there. Deep inside me, I felt encased in ice, fragile and off balance.

"We'll leave them here, with guards. I should ask Adam Nobel to post some as well. They'll be safer here. Far enough away that it will be far too difficult for the others to track them down. Junior and Master don't have the funds, and now the connections are drying up too."

If only sloughing off my fear was that simple. I needed a connection to remind me I was still alive, untainted by Haven and everything that had happened in my life. "Will you love me, Damien?"

"I'm not sure that's what you need," he said, and the well of anguish inside me changed into a flaming-hot mass of fury.

"I know what I want. You." I tugged the sheet away and threw myself from the bed, the nightgown my only covering. In my anger, I tore it, gripping the cloth so it pulled taut, then shredding the material down the centre. "I won't beg, Damien," I growled and advanced.

His gaze narrowed. "I will not treat you as an object, Ammy."

"No," I spat, "just withhold what I ask for. What I need."

He waited in silence as I moved forward, and I bared my teeth in a facsimile of a smile. "I'm here. Available. Naked. Take me."

His eyes jerked down and back up. "Yes, you're naked and beautiful. But you're also upset and—"

"Don't tell me what I am!" I shrieked.

He reached out and grabbed me, hauled me close as tears stung my eyes.

I railed and battered at him, my hands crashing against his back again and again. A furious rage engulfed me.

Damien held me until the emotions buffeting me bled away, and I slumped and sobbed in his embrace. "Why? Why did they do that to us? Use us? Sell us? Make us into nothing?"

"I don't know," he muttered. "But for all that, you made yourself into a courageous woman. Someone who cares and feels. Willing to take on children who aren't yours and protect them like a tigress."

I dug my fingers into his shirt and down to the flesh. I held on, needing him like a ship needed a rudder. "I don't want to remember."

"I know, Ammy. I'd take those memories if I could. I'd spare you the pain, but I can't."

"Is that why you won't love me?" I whispered.

His brow settled against mine. "No. I won't take advantage of you.

You're struggling, and I... I love you far too much to cheapen what's between us. I'll hold you tonight, if you wish. But I need to talk to you."

My gut clenched. I'd almost forgotten that he'd said we needed to talk. I looked down at my ruined gown and hauled it close around me. "I'm sorry. Let me change and—"

He stopped my words with a soft kiss. "No. Not that. Stay. Back under the covers and I'll explain."

"But my gown..." I bit my lip as a single tear escaped my lids.

"Take it off. Then under the covers."

I crawled under, and he tucked me in like a child. It felt odd to realise we'd been intimate so few times, yet I was unconcerned about my nudity with him. I'd have to reflect on that later, when my brain was capable of coherent thought.

"My people have been in touch. They think they know where Junior is. Master has returned to Haven. Going back presents its challenges, though I agree it's where we need to go next. We need to find Eldora, but we also need to interrogate Master, see what he knows."

"That's what you had to tell me?" I turned, shocked that it wasn't some big, bad, terrible thing.

"Yes... and no. They broke the perimeter barricade at the house. It's not destroyed but badly damaged. I have my people salvaging what they can, but..."

"What, Damien?"

"All my life, enforcement was what I wanted to do. My mother followed the path that was right for her, and I always thought that's what I was doing too. Now I wonder. When Adam Nobel said they had enforcement officers..." He sucked in an unsteady breath.

"Not the same as you," I added.

Damien nodded. "No, not the same, but still. If they're in his pocket, they've trampled their oath to humanity and justice."

I understood his dilemma. "And?"

"I need to contact the governor, explain what I've learned."

"Your superiors?"

He smiled now. "I don't have any actual superiors, Ammy. Did you look closely at my badge?"

I shook my head.

"I'm sheriff, yes, but more than that. The governor is who I report to. But both Andrew and I belong to a society of people who investigate and help those facing harm. We are not your average investigators. We carry all the same rights and authorities that local justice carry, but more as well. My mother was one of the first women to become members of the Extraordinary Judicial Enforcers."

I jerked upright. "What?"

"We're a covert arm of the government. My mother was recruited early because of her work as a physiotraducere. I joined once I left the rangers unit. I had the knowledge, skills, and connections after my mother's death. Andrew joined more recently. Most of us have family members affected by violence brought upon them by those who are enhanced."

"You mean with replacement limbs?"

"Yes, or eyes or any other part of themselves. Haven came to our notice through you and your brother. He was the first to work out that Haven was recruiting those with replacement limbs and amassing wives to build an army. After Eldora, we realised things were becoming unstable. It's why I came to Haven."

I swiped my hand over my eyes, weighing up everything he was saying. Haven wasn't the only place. "How many others?"

He shook his head. "We don't know. There aren't enough of us to police everywhere. We go where we're needed, though married members remain close to home."

"You need more. People with inside experience." My mind played with scenarios and ideas. "I could join—"

"No, Ammy. It's too dangerous." His gaze narrowed.

"Your mother knew. Who else? Gloriana?"

Damien winced, answering my question.

So, Gloriana was a member, yet I wasn't supposed to step up as well? Did he think me weak? "How do I join?" A hint of belligerence infused my question.

"Ammy..." he growled.

I waved an arm to stop him. "If you don't tell me, I'll ask Andrew or Gloriana."

His sigh, long and laboured, filled the air. "You have to meet the governor. He makes the determination."

"Fine. Then when this is settled, you'll make the introduction." I nestled down in the bed. "Now, come join me."

"Not..." Damien waved his arm.

"No, but perhaps in the morning. When you're feeling a little more settled."

The glint in his eyes took on a burning glow, but he shucked off his clothes, crawled naked into the bed, and hauled me close. "We'll discuss this in the morning."

He could discuss it till the cows came home, but I'd made my decision.

I snuggled in and closed my eyes, letting my body relax until I fell asleep.

The twitch of something hard against my skin woke me. I turned quietly, noting that Damien was still asleep, but the poking was the result of his erection.

I smiled.

Sliding my hand slowly beneath the covers, I found hot skin, a smattering of hair, and firm muscles. My hand continued to move as I gloried in the feel of the man beside me. I wanted to kiss the bared flesh, but he was still asleep, so I controlled myself, though just barely. I found the deep dip of his navel, circled it, then continued my pleasurable examination until my hand found an appendage. I slid my hand down its length, steel covered with velvet with a bulbed head. His cock was ready for action, with moisture beading the tip. I swallowed my gasp as my body heated and melted in reaction.

A sound rather like a soft grunt met my ears, and I looked up.

"I love you, Ammy," Damien whispered. During my short exploration, he'd woken, and I hadn't noticed, fully engrossed in exploring his body.

With careful moves, I straddled him. I'd heard wives talking of this form of congress, the pleasure it elicited for both members. With him, it felt right.

My legs rested on either side of his hips as I levered up. "I…"

He gripped my waist. "By all means," he said, eyes hot with wolfish pleasure.

I slid down, taking him inside me, feeling the stretching and filling.

"Damien," I moaned as he nudged at me.

"Control me, Ammy."

And I did, rising a little, then plunging down. The friction and caress of air against my now engorged nipples, the faint hint of coolness in direct counterpoint to the heat that amassed between my thighs.

"I love you, Damien." My head dropped back, boneless as I rode and undulated, taking and giving, needing and urging.

I'd been slick when I'd mounted him. Now I was wet and hot, melting and needing, and the only one who could make me whole was Damien.

My husband.

My lover.

He gripped my breasts, cupping them with gentle but eager movements, plucking at the nipples. The sensation shot through me, like lightning cracking through the sky.

The bed creaked as Damien urged our passion to fan hotter and flare brighter, and I cried out because it was beautiful and honest.

My body wound tight until I was there, hanging on the precipice of pleasure. Then I plunged, letting myself fall into the well where my body took control.

I knew when he'd climaxed, heard the groan of satisfaction and felt the hot spray of semen deep within. I gloried in it.

Then I slumped down, sated and so replete.

He wound his arms around me, holding us in that ultimate moment of oneness. He was still inside me, and I let the tears fall.

"Ammy? Did I hurt you?" His voice was thick with fear. Tension hardened his muscles, and he shoved at me.

I held on, needing him to stay where he was for a moment or two longer, unwilling to release him from the carnal embrace. "No. But it was beautiful. Like the perfection of the world is here, between us. No one else could possibly feel such pleasure," I whispered, trying to explain, though it was clumsy.

Damien relaxed once more. "Perfection is always you," he whispered as we kissed.

I laughed, a wet, snotty sound. "You have a way with words, Damien."

He wiped the tears from my face with unsteady fingers. "Only ever for you, Amaryllis Coultihan-Whitmore."

I snuggled down in the embrace. "I hadn't thought of that before. When we have children, we should call them that."

"If that's your wish, I am more than happy to assume the name."

I rose and looked at him. He smiled.

"Why?"

"Because I love you. If that's your wish, I would give in to it. I can't promise I'd give on everything, but that's a small, simple way of showing the wider world just how much I respect you. Who you are."

I wasn't sure that was what I wanted, but instead of worrying, I would think on it. Later.

I dozed, and when I woke, Damien was already gone.

Chapter Sixteen

The air held a nip, so I tugged my shawl close around me. The dirigible moved through the air, cutting a path quickly back to Haven. We'd left men and automative dogs behind, and while I didn't quite trust Adam Nobel, or his weird views on women and the world, he'd promised to watch over the children.

I turned to Andrew. "How much longer?"

He rolled his eyes. "We'll be in Haven tonight."

It wasn't quite an exact time, but for now I'd make do.

I marched to the end of the deck and glanced over the side. It was a long way down, and dizziness assailed me. I gripped the wooden rails and jerked away from the *whoosh whoosh whoosh* of the propeller. I'd already demanded an escorted examination of the control room and engineering bay. It was truly a wonder of modern technology, but it was the contents of the cargo bay that most captured my attention.

Within the cargo bay, I noted the rows of attack dogs and more than one highly fortified carriage. "What are they for?"

"If we're under attack, we can move at-risk subjects with speed," Andrew informed me, his face tight.

Some were pitted, and I realised for the first time that my brother had been involved in a few situations. He was obviously someone I really didn't know very well.

In a secured bay, I noted bandoliers, munitions, and weapons. Some made little sense, such as the wide snub-nosed rifle. I'd have to learn more.

We moved up to the main decks, which housed the men. They weren't luxurious, but bunks were neatly lined up with thick bedding ensuring their comfort, while tiny curtains gave them privacy. I noted the bathing rooms interspersing the larger rooms, with deep baths and new-fangled showers, where the water was forced into a low-slung head and jetted over the men below.

Traversing forward, I found a galley and dining room. "How many men have you transported on this?"

"Enough," he answered, and tempted though I was to roll my eyes at the non-answer, I kept it to myself.

On a higher deck were offices, his personal cabin, and two smaller ones, each with a private bathing room. There were also working areas and seating areas, though none could be described as large.

I'd counted around thirty men and only two other women aboard, but the ship seemed capable of housing many more. A cramped yet well-appointed medical bay rounded out the deck, and I shared my appreciation with Gloriana, who smiled. "Andrew is quite proud of his craft. It's still small, our fleet, but we're working to grow it."

I thought back to the small passenger transport he'd lost and was jolted by the knowledge that he was not just an inventor and transport-company mogul. That was simply the shell he allowed others to see. My brother, like my husband, was a man of layers.

"No wonder they seem to be good friends," I muttered.

"What was that, Ammy?" Gloriana asked.

I shook my head. "I don't see how they met. I mean, I can see why they're friends, but..."

"You know about Damien's mother, and the accident that killed his father. Your father was driven to ensure Andrew looked at the whole person when dealing with issues. He was ahead of his time, from what I understand. When Damien's father was killed, Andrew befriended him. They attended college together."

Still, there was so much I didn't know. Would I ever make my way through the many facets? Did I need to? I knew Damien on such an instinctive level already that maybe I didn't need to know it all.

"You should come inside now. Gloriana has arranged a meal for the four of us." Damien's hand snaked around my waist, and I threw off the memories.

"Yes, of course."

He laced my arm through his, and we descended into the belly of the ship. I excused myself to clean up and returned to find him waiting next to the dining table, the chair pulled out. I settled, and he slid the chair in behind me. The gentleman I'd never expected to find, let alone marry.

Over the meal of chicken and vegetables, cooked to perfection, Andrew shared what he'd learned.

"Master has taken up residence in the hotel. The women were sent to a farm some miles away."

I frowned. "Farm?" That jogged something in my memory, and I wondered if it could really be that simple.

"You remember something?" Damien's hand slid over mine.

"Yes. I mean, the money had to come from somewhere, right? I remember talk of yields and bales. Not a lot, because they didn't like to share information with the women, but... There's more than one farm." Now I looked up and glanced at Andrew. "Do you have access to a map?"

He nodded and hurried off, returning a few moments later. Gloriana cleared the table while Andrew, Damien, and I looked at the map.

"The meat was Haven's own. They would have a Thanksgiving meal annually. A sheep, a cow, and a pig were killed, the food cooked, and there'd be a large gathering of the household. Everyone had to attend. It happened just before Eldora came to live with us. I remember helping in the kitchen when the delivery arrived. I knew the face of one man. Caster Aldridge brought the carcasses inside. Made some remark about how good it must be to have food when others starved."

Andrew marked the map with an *X*. "Aldridge Farm is owned by HH Corporation."

HH Corporation. "Haven House," I breathed.

He looked at me. "The money trail you asked about? HH Corporation. There's more. Darren Smidwick and Francis Osmond also made regular deliveries."

Andrew noted them too. "I'll bet they're also owned by HH Corporation." He smiled. "I'd be willing to bet she's on one of those farms."

I bit my lip. "What if she isn't? There are plenty of places where you could hide a body." I looked at Damien.

"If she's not there, we'll find her, Ammy."

Gloriana cleared her throat. "Actually, I think there's another company. HH Corporation may be the shell used by the sect, but my father isn't a man who'd leave something like this to chance, nor his own personal comforts. There'll be at least one more, maybe two. We should check the list of company names registered in the state. They'll be some kind of amalgam of names, I would think."

Andrew grunted. "You could be right. Damien, I need you to have your men look into the HH Corporation, see who is listed as trustee or directors."

Damien nodded and pulled out his communicase, tapping out the request. "It will take time."

Now Gloriana cleared her throat. "I may have snuck into his office once or twice when I was younger and looking for things. He kept a notebook." I stared at my sister-in-law. "A small black-and-red one where he kept information he deemed important. If we could find it…"

Andrew's grin widened. "Yes, of course, my love." He took her face in both hands and kissed her soundly before us. Never had I seen the casualness of such affection. I'd come across them embracing since I'd left Haven House, but none of them had been expected. This here, it reminded me of Damien and our relationship.

I bit my lip and turned slightly. Damien took my hand, and I glanced up at him, read the understanding of how flustered I felt.

"When we land, we'll head to the house. It'll be better if we travel on horseback. No engines to give away our presence, and the terrain isn't conducive to using the machines anyway."

Chapter Seventeen

I dressed in the pants and shirt Damien brought to me. It felt oddly constricting around my legs but also freeing, my movements unhampered by gowns, petticoats, and such other apparel. I bent to slide on the boots he'd given me, the laces strange, but Damien bent down and tied them. "Now you're ready."

I glanced at the looking glass. He'd already instructed me to tie my hair back and up. He wound his arms around my waist, dragging me back, his face pale. "You stay at the rear, no matter what happens. We know Master has men with him, enforcers. They'll see you as a target, and that I can't allow."

"I'll stay out of the way, and when the time is right, Gloriana and I will retrieve the notebook."

He prowled the room, a caged lion, and I moved to him, taking his hands. "I won't take chances, my love."

His gaze blanked for a moment. "I won't lose you, Ammy."

A rattle caught our attention. "Miss Ammy? Sheriff? Your presence is required downstairs in the office," called Aloysius from the other side of the door.

I took Damien's hand, and we left the room, both of us aware of the dangers of the mission ahead. I just hoped I'd be able to assist and not become a thorn in his side.

We entered the library, and I noted Gloriana was dressed in trousers as well. Glasses sat on a tray filled with a ruby liquid. "Come," she said. "We'll drink a toast and prepare."

I took the glass offered to me and sipped. It was heady liquid, full-bodied, and I replaced it on the tray, waiting for Andrew to explain how we would achieve the final outcome.

He'd drawn a small map of the town, showing the hotel at the very end, nearest the hill where Haven House stood, now empty.

"Damien, you'll lead a contingent directly to the house. Enter via the rear. Ten men and three automative dogs on silent. Their handlers are non-combatant, hence not included in the count, and I'll send them in fortified carriages. You go in, secure the premises only. We'll search later."

Andrew cleared his throat, and Damien nodded. "They may clear out—"

"That's why it's imperative to round up their men. I'll take a second team and storm the hotel. We take Master alive. He's got much to answer for. Once he's secured, we send Gloriana and Ammy in. They secure the notebook. With that, we then take a smaller third contingent and move to the farm. We search for and hopefully secure the remains of Eldora."

It sounded easy to hear Andrew say it, but fear was forming a yawning pit in my stomach.

"What if we don't find the notebook on him?" I asked.

Gloriana placed a hand on my shoulder. "He always has it with him. I'm sure we'll retrieve it easily."

The others finished their glasses, and we left the office. By now, the men and machines would be waiting for us.

The horses snuffled as we mounted. It felt odd to be atop a horse once more. I hadn't ridden in years, but the practical knowledge returned swiftly, and I took up the reins and followed the others down the driveway.

Night was drawing in. I shivered beneath the oilskin coat I wore, but we travelled swiftly, the groups Andrew had decreed forming as we closed in on the town.

Before he left, Damien grabbed me close. "I love you, Ammy. So stay safe, because we have many happy years ahead of us once we're done here."

My eyes pricked. "You too, my love." I knew my voice sounded thick, but I couldn't help it. Terror nipped at me as I watched him in the light of the lamp he carried. That would be extinguished soon, but I followed it for as long as I could.

Then it winked out.

Gloriana's horse sidestepped and whinnied. "We should move out of sight," she whispered, and I followed her into the shadow of the closest building. The bank.

The town wasn't big, but we could find locations that would hide us from view as Andrew, badge now pinned to his chest, rode up the main street. He didn't extinguish his lamp.

Nerves bit at me. How simple would this truly be?

Two men appeared at the end of the laneway, and I grabbed Gloriana's hand. "Men coming."

She turned her head, spotted them, and dug her heels into the side of her horse. I followed suit, and we burst from our cover and rode closer to the action. This was not where Andrew wanted us, but I didn't question her movements. She'd been trained, Andrew had explained, and I hadn't.

But if I trusted my gut, it would tell me this was not where we needed to be.

Shouts echoed in the air. Gunshots.

My heart stilled, then began beating again, faster than before, as if it wished to jump from my chest.

Lights illuminated the hotel. Voices and screams. Demands.

Then a gunshot.

Just one.

"We need to get in there," Gloriana told me as she slid down from the saddle. "Quickly now," she urged, and I followed her forward after we'd secured the horses to the railing.

The door of the hotel hung drunkenly on a single hinge. I stared at it. The building had always been perfectly cared for. This was a reminder that we were about to change something I'd known my whole life. It didn't matter that it was for the better, that we would save other women the indignities I'd shared with them.

We pushed inside, and I noted the huddle of women on the floor. Some I knew. "It's all right," I called. "Stay there and you'll be safe."

A head peered over the balustrade of the staircase. "What are you...?"

Feet clattered down the stairs, and we were pulled to the side. "He's gone," one of Andrew's men muttered.

Gloriana's gaze locked with mine. "My husband?"

"Upstairs searching." His terse answer came quickly. "Round up the women and get them outside."

Here was something I could do. I hurried back to the main room. "We need to go outside," I told them.

Voices rose as they questioned and queried.

"Why should we?" It was a voice I knew well. One of Master's earlier wives. She was loud and demanding.

"Because it's in your best interests," I answered, and she scoffed.

I knew some women and called them by name. A few rose and hurried for the door.

Gloriana had disappeared, and I was here on my own with a bunch of women who had no intentions of leaving.

Anger rose in me, wild and deep. "Get up!" I bellowed. The woman who'd questioned me just blinked. "Now!"

They did, mouths slack.

"Outside. Form a group in the roadway. Sit down and wait." I spoke with a firmness I'd never used before used. But my nerves were shredding, because I didn't know what was happening. All I knew was they needed these women to obey.

They did, although more than one muttered under her breath, calling me a harlot and unbeliever. I didn't let the verbal arrows find a soft place to land.

Once they were out, I glanced back and saw Gloriana, her face white. I hurried to her.

"What?"

"We found him. Dead. He'd been choked and hidden in a cupboard. I checked, and there's no notebook!"

My mind spun. She'd been so sure! "Have you checked drawers, cupboards?"

Gloriana nodded. "Yes. I need you to go to the house, Ammy. Find Damien and search there. He must have hidden it."

I nodded and shot from the building, my feet pelting down the wooden veranda and onto the ground.

I grabbed the reins and mounted the horse, my brain and heart urging me to speed.

I rode full tilt to the house. Once more, I tied the horse to the rail just beyond the house and then hurried up the stairs I hated so much. I thrust the door open and saw a sight that froze everything in my brain and chest.

A man, face down.

I knew him. He was an enforcer.

"Damien?" I called, then heard racing footsteps and the growl of the dogs. Automative dogs, capable of tearing a person limb from limb.

I glanced upward. On the stairs lying across the steps was another body. Scarlet ribbons adorned his chest, eyes blank and wide open. I ran up them, heading to the rooms where Master had lived. I hoped I'd find Damien alive.

The scent of copper grew stronger, and I heard grunts and the sound of flesh striking flesh.

Another growl as I rounded a corner to find three men, backs to the wall, eyes wide with terror. More enforcers.

"We'll get you!" one of them shouted at me.

I ignored them and searched, eyes wide and hair escaping from the tight braid, almost blinding me. I shoved the strands aside and hurried for Master's room. The door was painted in scarlet. My hands circled the frigid silver knob. It turned beneath my touch. I entered the room, and there was Damien, three men before him.

One lunged, and I clamped my lips together, not wanting to surprise Damien, because they'd kill him. I knew it.

A man lay upon the floor, another of Andrew's men, his hand pressed against a wound in his belly, but it still bled copiously. He'd need help quickly if he were to survive. He caught my eye, and I nodded. As soon as I could safely do so, I'd be there.

Damien circled, knife in hand and the glow of his badge bright in the lamplight.

The three men laughed and horsed around as they also circled.

One feinted, and Damien slashed out.

The man jumped back, and another lunged. A swift movement from Damien and he was on the floor, rolling and holding the area between his legs, shrieking.

One down, but the other two still danced against Damien.

His eyes were hard, searching, and I watched the way his muscles bunched and strained. The third made a move, and Damien was there, ploughing his fist into the man's face. Blood spurted into the air, and the man dropped, howling, to the floor.

One remaining combatant against Damien.

I held my breath. *Please, God. Please!* The entreaty became a refrain that ran over and over in my mind.

This man wasn't weak like the others. He moved in to attack, fists and feet flying.

Damien retreated, the knife flashing.

Again the man advanced, and Damien's face hardened.

The sound of metal flying through the air.

Then sudden stillness.

Damien had tossed the knife, and it found a home embedded in the man's eye. He stopped, grunted, then, as if his legs could no longer hold him, crumpled to the floor.

Damien turned. "Dammit, what are you doing here?"

I brushed past him, dropping to my knees by the injured team member. "Master's dead. No sign of the notebook at the hotel. I was sent here to look because I know the layout."

My hands moved quickly now, tearing at the man's shirt, and Damien crouched beside me. "How bad?"

I moved the man's hands and hissed. "Very. Get him outside to the carriage. He's going to need the physician if there's any hope of saving him. Send someone to me, but I'll begin searching in here."

While I spoke, I bundled up the shredded remains of the shirt and stuffed them tightly into the wound. "I'll pack this first, get the pressure on. You get him downstairs."

I scurried into the bedroom, not stilling to check out the enormous bed but instead going immediately to the wardrobe and taking out three shirts. As I returned to the sitting room, I started tearing them into strips.

I hunkered down beside the injured man. "I'm going to tie this around you. It'll hurt, but we need pressure right now."

My hands were slick with blood, but I quickly had the makeshift bandages in place, then moved out of the way so Damien could lift him.

Men raced into the room, members of Andrew's team. They took control of the two on the floor, and I moved on autopilot, tearing out each drawer and hunting for the book. The sitting room didn't hold the item I was hunting for, so I entered the bedroom again and finally allowed myself to look over what I saw.

"Where would you hide something like that?" I'd already seen inside the wardrobe, but the shelf at the top was possible. I tugged all the clothing out, and when it lay on the floor, there was still no book. I tossed the bed, emptied every drawer.

Nothing.

I turned in a slow circle. "Where?"

A glint caught my eye, and I advanced. The bed head sat oddly, more than a little off-centre, and I reached over and slid my hand down. A panel caught my hand. "Dammit!"

I jerked at it, and the panel came away. A dirty, slightly dusty hidey-hole was revealed.

There it lay—the book. Black and red, just as Gloriana had said.

Only there wasn't just one. There were three, plus a sheaf of papers and something else. I grabbed them all and looked for a bag.

None!

I tore a case off a pillow and shunted the items deep into it, then tied it to my belt, thinking I may yet need my arms free.

I slid over the mountain of detritus that littered the floor, then wrenched the bedroom door open.

A rumble began toward the back of the building, and I stilled, wondering what it might be.

The floorboards beneath my feet started dancing and jostling up and down. Wide-eyed, I looked around. Smoke, thick and greasy, rose through the floorboards and from the doors. But there was really only one way out of the building. I coughed, choking on the silent plumes of grey smoke.

A thud sounded, louder than before, then another. Getting closer.

Blood surged in my veins.

"I need to get out of here," I muttered and reached for the door, but it was hot. My hand was seared in contact with the metal knob, and I screamed with the pain. I hauled it back, cradling the damaged appendage against my belly.

Horror filled me.

If I don't get out now, I may never. The reality rode me hard, the tiny hairs at the nape of my neck standing on end.

"Move!" I shouted at myself.

Another boom echoed in the air.

The building shuddered beneath my feet, and I stumbled hard. Plaster rained down, and I fell to my knees with another crack. "Oh my God!" I lurched back up, turned for the window, but before I could reach it, a thunderous boom sounded, and things started falling from the walls and the ceiling.

A large light fixture crashed down, sending up shards of glass, and I raised my arms to protect my face.

Darkness descended on the room, and something heavy whacked me from behind. I landed on the floor, the weight and pain warring to capture my attention.

My body spasmed as I screamed in terror and agony. It radiated throughout my body, and I arched up. I didn't know what pinned me, just that it hurt. So bad!

"Damien!"

That one last word escaped before darkness claimed me.

Chapter Eighteen

The hard surface beneath me was moving. Bouncing.

Every movement jarred my body. My head felt as if it were splitting in two.

I fought to stay awake, because the hand holding mine was warmer than I was.

"Damien," I moaned before the darkness captured me once more.

Opening my eyes was like climbing a mountain. An effort of will and determination.

The walls were white, and I was sure I'd seen it before, but where? It was a question I couldn't quite grasp the answer to.

My lips were dry, cracked, my mouth raspy and tight. "Water," I groaned.

A cloth was slipped between my lips, and I sucked weakly.

When it was removed, I lay back, my body exhausted from the simple effort.

"Ammy?"

I couldn't turn my head, but I knew the voice. "Damien."

I felt his hand on mine, the grip tight. His face swam into view, lined and grey. Exhausted.

"Where am I?"

"Aboard the dirigible. You needed the facilities here." Pain, bare and deep, echoed in the verdant green of his eyes.

"What happened?" My voice was soft and faint, as if coming from far away.

"There was a fail-safe. They detonated the building while you were..." His eyes fluttered shut, and when they reopened, the pools of pain were near infinite. "They nearly killed you, Ammy." Tears glittered in his eyes.

"I thought they did." I moved slightly, and the agony I felt was incomparable. "I hurt. My leg hurts," I murmured.

He blanched. "Ammy, your leg..." The grip on my hand tightened.

"Did I hurt it badly?" My mouth was dry again. I licked my lips, and he slid the sponge in once more. The moisture dribbled down my throat as I sucked deeply, welcoming the water.

When he removed it from my mouth, he turned away. I heard him gulp and wondered what was so bad that he was afraid to face me.

"Damien?"

Misery and guilt contorted his face when he looked back at me. "They had to amputate it. At the knee."

I stared at him, blank. The things he was saying...

Amputate.

"No," I whispered. "No."

"Yes. They had to do that to get you out of there. The building was on fire, and there was no other option." His hand shook on my cheek. "You would have died, Ammy."

I wanted to jerk away but couldn't because I was immobile on the bed. Every word was a spike into the centre of my brain.

My leg. I was no longer whole. *Damaged.*

"But I'll organise a physiotraducere, Ammy. The best, if that's what you want. You don't need to decide now."

His earnest tone was too much to bear. I closed my eyes, trying to understand all he'd told me.

My leg. *Gone.*

The pain remained.

I was sure I could feel it.

Perhaps it was a joke? Cruel, but in a moment, he'd laugh...

I waited, heart pounding, but it didn't echo in the air, and on some level, I knew.

"Ammy?" I heard it, the sorrow.

Too much!

The pounding in my head swelled, and I let go of consciousness.

Day and night ceased for me that day. There was only the agony of awareness or the darkness that stole me into nothingness.

Every time I opened my eyes, Damien was there. His hand in mine, holding tight, as if my anchor. I supposed on some level he was, but why stay now? Now that I wasn't normal. Never again would I be.

Gradually, I came back to myself once more and met the doctor who'd saved my life after the wild flight back to Scottsvale. That was where they'd transported me to, because the hospital facilities were better, Damien informed me. The black cloud settled around me, cloaking me. Smothering me.

I wasn't yet ready to see what was no more. I avoided it, until after my release from the hospital and on the trip back to what had become our home in Port Alino. Damien strode into the room, Gloriana and Andrew at the door. His eyes were dark-rimmed, and stubble coated his jaw. His clothes were rumpled in a way I'd never before seen.

He'd lost weight. Guilt nibbled at the corners of my despair. "Damien?"

"Enough, Ammy. Time to get up. Time to get some air." His tone was belligerent and his gaze direct. I hadn't seen that from him in a long while, it seemed.

My body seized up. "I don't want..." I muttered.

His shoulders tensed. "Too bad. Now come on."

Gloriana brought in a chair, a contraption with wheels, and set it by my bed, her gaze darting back and forth.

Damien reached down and scooped me up, pulling the blanket with me. "Come on."

The warmth I associated with him returned, filling my body, which now felt chilled and lifeless.

"Put me back," I demanded with a quaver, but he ignored me. Once I was settled into the chair, he tucked the surrounding covers down the sides. I stared straight forward, refusing to acknowledge that I now only had one and a half legs.

The squeak of the wheels attacked my ears. We trundled out, and he took me to the front of the dirigible. A pulley on a platform awaited me. A lift, I'd heard it called.

The chains pulled tight, and we rose.

Sunlight seared me, burning my eyes. Pressure filled me. I fought it down, suppressed it as best I could.

A salty breeze tousled my hair. I glanced around, but the railings were too high. I pursed my lips. "I want to go back," I muttered with a mulish insistence.

They ignored me.

I knew something was up. As soon as the rattle and clank of chains started, the dirigible started dropping.

I gawked. "What's going on?"

"We're almost home, Ammy. Back to where the children are waiting for us."

Children. Francesca, Simeon, Samson, Faith, and Constance.

I bit my lip. "Are they safe?"

Damien crouched beside me. "Yes. But they need us. They need you, Amaryllis Coultihan-Whitmore. You're their mother now."

A chink of need etched its way through the frozen organ in my chest. Heat moved down my face, and I swiped at my cheek, surprised to find moisture. A tear.

"No," I said.

"Amaryllis. You are not broken. I love you."

I looked at him. "How? I'm broken. A shell." And I meant it.

"No." He brushed a lock of hair from my face. "You're my life. The light that makes me whole."

My chest heaved as emotions swirled within me, threatening to swamp me. I clasped my fingers, dug deep with my nails. "Why?"

His gaze held mine. "Because you are the woman who sees me. Knows me. Accepts me. Just as I see you and accept you."

A sob tore through the air, loud and wild. The sound of an animal in pain, I realised. But it was me.

His arms enfolded me, held me close as I allowed the dam to burst. Let the horror, pain, sorrow, and regrets rise to the surface.

"I don't want to be broken, Damien." I wept into the shoulder of his jacket while the beat of his heart and the heat of him applied a balm to my wounded soul.

"I won't let you be. When you're ready, we'll find a doctor. You set the rules, Ammy. Only you."

D
earest Diary,

Amaryllis Coultihan-Whitmore is still the strongest woman I know.

Since the night we found Master of Haven House dead, she's been to hell and back.

Since that night, Damien has been a rock to her and to us. Working with her hasn't been easy. She's grieved the loss of her leg. We all know it was necessary to save her. She's accepted that now, but we feared we'd lose her to the blackness of spirit. It nearly stole her.

Since then, the surgeries have been successful. We're all thankful, because it's given her back the life she lost that night.

Today we received news that another shining light entered the world. Dawn Coultihan-Whitmore was born, healthy and well, just as her mother is.

Francesca has blossomed as well during this time. Her drive and tenaciousness have seen her enter medical training, and she's indicated her chosen field is that of Physiotraducere, carrying on what could very well be a tradition in the family.

Damien assures us that Francesca, Faith, Constance, Samson, and Simeon are all overjoyed at the birth of a little sister.

I can't wait to introduce my little Alexander to Dawn. He's still too *young yet to realise that he was born into a world that allows him to be who and whatever he wants to be. That will come in time.*

I have also heard that the man we know as Adam Nobel has passed from this life.

While I can never condone the life he lived or the sect he led, I remain grateful to this day for his care of the children during one of the most trying times of our lives.

I can only hope that, our duty being done, we may now settle into a peaceful life.

Then again, I doubt it!

We shall see, though.

Gloriana Mulligan-Coultihan

The End

...for now

Francesca's story will come soon in *Nobel Crest*.

When Cupid—otherwise known as Diocail— is banished from his home on a remote Scottish Island, he's set a series of tasks by the great god Lugh, who also happens to be his father.

In **Blame The Wine**, he must bring two lovers together... BBW Cara and James, the man she's lusted over from afar who happens to be a super geek and head Veha Industries.

In **A Stranger's Embrace**, Diocail is driven to help an emotionally fragile Jane and Davis, a famous author. The task is more complicated, with the existence of Carstairs her could-be ex-husband and teenage daughter, Frannie.

In **Revenge on Cupid**, Diocail must take the ultimate chance and find his own happily ever after with Simone. Sometimes the past gets in the way and HEA's don't come cheap though.

The dusty, dingy little diner was full, even with its current state of cleanliness—or lack thereof. People from the surrounding offices didn't care about anything except the incredible, well-prepared food at a reasonable cost. They flooded in, like waves to the shore. As one tide left, another swept in.

"Honestly, Simone. I'm going to try getting his attention one more time. If that doesn't work, I'm out of there. I mean, how long can I keep trying?" Cara picked at the caramel tart she hadn't been able to resist with the cheap metal fork and flicked the blob of fresh cream that sat on top to the side of the plate.

"You've said that tons of times before. Besides, what are you going to do to get his attention? Hmm? Walk naked through the typing pool?" Simone bobbed the straw in her smoothie as she eyed her friend with a frown. "It's been what? Eighteen months since you saw him, and you've mooned over him from a distance ever since you met him. You need to move on, Cara. That is, unless there's something you haven't shared?"

The query was arch. Cara shivered even as she shook her head. "No."

Simone quirked an eyebrow, obviously unconvinced with the answer. Cara let out a deep sigh of frustration. "There's a position...it's only temporary, for a PA reporting directly to him." She speared a forkful of tart, chewed quickly and swallowed, before continuing. "In his office, full-time for the period of the engagement. I saw the memo yesterday. I mean, I have the skills, right? I can type, answer phones, make coffee, file, greet people. What's more, I can probably do it better than all those size eights in the typing pool that Ms. Jackman seems to prefer." She nodded thoughtfully. "All I have to do is get past the ogre in Human Resources."

Simone stared at her, disbelief clear on her face. "Girl, I so remember that woman. If you think you can get past her, you're doing better than I ever did. That's why I left Veha Industries, remember? Maybe it's time to haul out your resumé and consider some other options. Look for something better." Simone shook her head and billows of her crimson hair swirled through the still air.

Cara understood Simone only had her best interests at heart. But this time she knew the outcome would be different. Hell, she could feel it in the air. The tingle of expectation.

"Cara, the HR ogre will hang you out for breakfast before she offers you anything like a position in that office. Remember her mantra? Good looks and good work make for a positive workplace!"

Simone didn't sugar-coat anything. It was another great reason for their long- term friendship. Honesty. But Cara didn't want to hear the truth in the statement. Even if it was exactly as her friend said.

Cara nodded quickly. "Yeah, I know, but if I don't try, then I won't know how close I can get to him, right? And the only way to catch his attention is to get past *her* and see him in person." Cara quaked a little at the information she needed to share. The favor she needed to ask. "Anyway, I tidied up my resumé and dropped the application into a memo envelope yesterday, so it's too late to back out now. I mean, fortune favors the brave. Doesn't it? If I don't snag an interview, I'm going to visit the career advisor across the street and register with them." She shrugged. "I'll look for temp work until something more long-term shows up. I can see what they have on offer and well...who knows? Maybe a job with the right boss is just waiting for me. But I'd rather this worked out, to be honest." Her voice trailed off into a whisper. "I really wish he would notice me."

Simone took a long slurp of her banana drink, and Cara noticed her questioning gaze even as she squirmed. Finally, Simone nodded. "It's your funeral. So anyway, you'd better show me this memo if you want me to be a referee for you. I'm guessing that's what you need, right? I'll have to know what I'm supposed to say about you before they ring."

Cara smiled. "Thanks, Simone. I knew I could count on you." She slipped a piece of paper out of her handbag and handed it over. "Sorry it's a bit creased. It was in the bottom of my bag, I stashed it so none of the others from the pool would see. You know how it is."

Available from Love Books Publishing
books2read.com/CelticCupid

Direct Autographed Copy
https://www.imogenenix.net/CelticCupid

Star of Ishtar

Warriors of the Elector
Book One

The first time Elara laid eyes on Grayson was when he rescued her from the clutches of a madman and his scientists who were kidnapping humans and conducting horrific experiments on them. That was years ago. In spite of her attempts to deepen their relationship, they remained nothing more than close friends.Now Elara is a medic with the Admiralty, and she knows what she wants. It's been Grayson since the beginning. When Elara is stationed on the *Star of Ishtar*, she arrives with a plan to further her career. But this time her plan has an added bonus—to finally get her man.

Grayson's spent years fighting the connection between himself and Elara. He's certain it only exist because he saved her life. But his will is failing, and he fears he just might give in to temptation.

"I finally made it." Elara Sudonne watched as the hull of the *Star of Ishtar* loomed in the inky darkness. She clutched her hands tightly together as the shuttle approached the hulking battleship.

This would be her new home and first combat ST placement for the Earth Empire. She quaked inwardly with nerves but fought to keep her serene exterior. Previously her deployments had consisted solely of on-planet expeditions and in rehabilitation and dirtside facilities. When the chance had arisen to move to the battleship, she'd grabbed it with both hands.

The frigid air chilled her bones as she sat in her shuttle seat, but a trickle of sweat inched its way down her back under the fresh gray wool flight uniform. Little puffs of vapor escaped her mouth as she rubbed her arms. Nerves stretched tight, she looked through the small portal at the front of the vessel. She wanted to tug at the collar that somehow seemed to have grown tighter as the ship loomed ahead, but instead she firmed her mouth, straightened her spine, and concentrated on the future.

"So damned long." She'd been working toward this outcome since the day Grayson Myatt and Duvall McCord had saved her from her Ru'Edan captors. She was lucky, she'd survived the 'experimentation' of the Ru'Edan leader Crick Sur Banden's scientists. "And all I have to remind me are my scars." She didn't grin at her own joke.

The person seated behind her jostled but she ignored it, lost in her memories. On that day, so very long ago, the young Elara, fresh-faced and with idealistic views of the empire, was taken from the mall where she'd been shopping with friends, thrust into the back of a transport vehicle, and given to the Ru'Edan scientists to experiment on.

For days they'd worked on her and others, seeking an average pain threshold of humans, slicing her skin then noting reactions and how long it took to heal. They'd cut her arms, body, and even her face, and now she carried the extensive scarring of the exercise as a reminder to herself and others of what they were fighting for. Freedom. The freedom of Earth and its allied planets.

She'd never relinquished hope, it had been her constant companion as she fought against the all-consuming terror. Then they'd found her in that dirty, disused warehouse. They'd found others too, in various states of death and decay. The smells of despair had filled the air with a fetid ripeness that she'd never been able to forget.

Since that day she'd promised herself that she would pay the Ru'Edan back for what they'd done to her. What they'd taken from her. Over the years, she tempered and honed the rage while remaining adamant that she would see the final act played out. She couldn't physically fight, but she had learned about trauma, knew it and understood how it affected a person, and used it as a weapon.

The iron will forged through her experiences had fed her determination, and she'd applied herself to study, finishing in the top ten percent of her class. She entered the medical program at the academy, working hard to excel. Her family remained supportive if perplexed as to why she had chosen to keep reminding herself of what had happened.

The maw of the *Star of Ishtar* loomed closer, opening its cavernous mouth as she watched through the portal. She could hear the voices of the shuttle crew signaling their intention to enter and land, the tinny confirmation coming swiftly. She watched avidly while the shuttle maneuvered, imagining the invisible shields dropping to allow it entry.

Her hands twisted with fear and anger, but she tamped down her emotions. Anger never helped anyone. Staying strong, knowing your history, and ensuring it couldn't be repeated, they were the answers, she told herself firmly, pulling herself from the grip of a dark past so horrific she still saw it in her dreams. She pushed it away to the recesses of her mind and focused on what she was about to do.

A squark overhead, the usual mechanical sound that alerted all on board to a transmission by the captain, caught her attention. "Attention all passengers. We are entering the shuttle bay. Please ensure when you disembark you remove all personal items. Move beyond the white line and wait for your designation."

The lights of the bay flashed as they entered, and once again Elara marveled at how far humanity had moved since they had first walked the Earth. She saw the opening of the structure as the shuttle moved into the bay, inching forward slowly until it stopped its ponderous motion and began its descent to the floor. Something deep inside warmed even as the shuttle's environmental systems began to synchronize with the cooler temperature of the *Star of Ishtar*, and she felt a smile crawl its way over her face.

Elara breathed in deeply, inhaling the metallic-tasting, recycled air and welcoming the calmness that settled on her body. Her eyes closed as she filled her lungs. "I'm here." There was more than a little satisfaction in her tone, and she smiled. She slowly exhaled, finding that center of peace she relied on.

A loud thud and clank echoed as the deep drone split the air. The engines were powering down, and there she was, on one of the Earth Empire's Emeritus class battleships. She sat in her seat, waiting for the all clear from the captain, and once it sounded through the cabin, she rose, tugging at the webbing belt and disengaging it.

The small backpack beside her was all she carried as she made her way to the exit, not needing to duck as so many others did. She stepped through the door, her hands gripping the rail of the cold, metal stairs which connected to the side of the gray shuttle.

She clambered down them slowly, savoring the experience. The sting of the cold on her hands from the stairs, frigid from even their brief exposure to the blackness of space, made her flinch inwardly. The shuttle journey from the Admiralty's strategic base at Aenna to their current position had taken just over an hour, but the whole time it felt like her heart had been in her throat. Her mouth was dry as she followed the new recruits from the ship into the landing bay. She stopped, silently noting the slight mustiness of the air, the recycled quality easily recognizable. Everything, including the oxygen, needed recycling in space.

All around her people swarmed, either around the ships or into the dogleg line that now formed ahead of her. Someone had opened the baggage locker of the shuttle, and the sound of dropping bags hitting the plascrete floor echoed in the air. Another crewmember guided trolleys to the other side of the shuttle, pulling out boxes with important day-to-day items for the ship, including vaccines and plants. She watched briefly, all the while listening to the alien cacophony. Voices called in welcome to old crewmembers, while new ones watched, many goggle-eyed in the fresh uniforms of newly minted officers and crewmembers.

Her gaze flicked around quickly, taking in the sights, sounds, and smells, pungent with oils and grease; burning smells from the scorched plascrete and the press of sweaty or nervous bodies. She joined the line silently, tacking onto the end, and stayed at parade rest, knowing the welcoming voice would cut through the air soon enough. She felt somehow disconnected from the main throng. Perhaps the knowledge that this was the outcome she had worked for years to achieve set her apart. However, still, she felt so...distant from everything around her. She smiled secretly at the bout of whimsy.

"Attention!" The voice boomed out over the plascrete of the docking bay, and she snapped her body into position, noting the commander who had bellowed the words. Technically, she outranked most members aboard the *Star of Ishtar*, except for the command and leadership staff, but she knew all newcomers had to join the welcoming parade, regardless of rank.

Fleet Captain Elphin came into view, his tired features topped by salt-and-pepper gray hair, which highlighted his cool blue eyes. Elara also recognized a body prone to a little middle-aged thickness. Following behind him was his second-in-command, Duvall McCord. A young up-and-coming officer, his status as a fast-tracking officer heading toward his own command, with Elphin both his mentor and captain, had become almost legendary at the academy.

She looked closely at McCord, noting the dynamic drive of his actions and movements. Soon he would achieve a promotion to captain, and she rejoiced for her friend. She'd followed his career with interest and had to tamp down a smile as his eyes betrayed the shock of seeing her before settling into their flat command persona. So he hadn't been apprised of her deployment, she noted, and she had to restrain the tiny feeling of surprise and satisfaction. She filed that snippet of information away.

She caught sight of the man standing behind Duvall. Grayson Myatt. He'd made her heart beat faster for years. Tall and blond with a muscular build and a sexy, tight, little butt, he had pools of deep-blue eyes that had always made her think of forever. He had a growth of stubble on his chiseled jaw, and her fingers itched to touch his perfect lips. Yes, since the day he'd found her in that nasty warehouse tied down like a ragged animal, she'd worshipped him from afar.

Now she had her opportunity to tangle with him, hopefully much closer than any chance that had ever come her way before. With a sigh, she pulled her gaze back to the captain and forced herself to concentrate on his words. She couldn't afford to have her commanding officer angry due to her being distracted.

"Welcome to the *Star of Ishtar*. Most academy recruits want to join us because of what we represent, but on this ship, we only take the best of the best. So, if you made it here, you're the ones we wanted to take a look at. Getting here is only the first step. Staying here is harder to achieve. Our people are the best. Earn your place, and in return, we'll make you one of our crew—a member of the *Star of Ishtar*. Only the best and the brightest wear our uniform and badge. You'll be expected to perform to your absolute limit then give some more. We don't tolerate people who don't pull their weight. Do us proud and wear your uniform with pride." The captain looked out over the new members of his crew. His voice had echoed during his speech, and now it died away.

He scanned the faces before him, and she could almost read his thoughts. There were new security officers and a smattering of other crew. Some of them were young and impressionable, and she knew a few wouldn't make the cut as crewmembers. Others would carve out their place on the *Star of Ishtar* and move to better positions and placements, like she would: the new SurgiTech, a younger female, experienced but untried on board a ship. She smiled at that thought.

Some of those who stood with her would be replaced as they failed the exacting standards the captain set. She'd heard that he was a firm captain, fair but demanding. He'd have to be to command this ship. The

Ishtar had well over five hundred at full capacity, and the captain could select their placements as his command staff saw fit from the many who applied to join the crew. She sensed his satisfaction with the choices in the relaxation of his body.

Abruptly, he turned to Duvall, breaking her study of him. "Get them to where they need to present themselves." His words echoed as he walked away. He had a purposeful stride. Quick but unhurried, like he knew where he was going and how to get there. A man who knew how to get what he wanted. Someone to respect and admire.

"My name is Commander Duvall McCord. I am your second-in-command, and my direct subordinate is Commander Grayson Myatt. While you are aboard the *Star of Ishtar* you will be required to fulfill your duties efficiently. As Captain Elphin said, do your job right and you will be one of ours, with all the benefits that come with being a crewmember of the *Star of Ishtar*."

He paused and eyeballed each of the newer recruits, those fresh from the academy. Many of them paled under his gaze, and she smiled inwardly. Even the older people in the line seemed to quake beneath his scowl. He'd always had that air of innate authority, even when barely out of the academy himself. She knew his methods and watched him make full use of the carefully practiced tone of presence.

"Each of you has been assigned. You will present yourselves to the chief of your section. Those details will be found in your orders. Commander Myatt has organized a team to escort you to your cabins. You will have approximately one hour to prepare. We've arranged for crewmembers to escort you to your superiors. Be ready to present for duty. Any issues, you will, of course, take up with your section commander. Should there be need to take any further action, you will see Commander Myatt. You should only see me if you are a command crewmember or as a point of discipline. I am not one for small talk, so if you present to me, have a very good reason."

He delivered the words slowly and deliberately, and Elara restrained a small smile on hearing at least one gulp from those in the line nearest her.

"We run a tight ship here. Discipline and commitment are the two key factors we look for beyond loyalty in our crew. You will from henceforth represent our ship everywhere, and we do not tolerate anything less than the best." He looked around once more, the stern demeanor he wore so well reinforcing the message. If she hadn't known him for so long, she too might have missed the hint of humor glinting in his eyes, the one many took for coldness.

Her legs ached, and she wanted to move and relieve the pressure on them, but she held herself still, waiting for the command to dismiss. She wouldn't let herself or him down now. Not after she'd worked so long to achieve this position.

As the new ST, she had no previous experience on ships. She had vast experience in the field, but Elara was aware that would count for little in the eyes of most of the crew. She didn't intend to signal a weakness to anyone and least of all on her first day aboard the *Star of Ishtar*. That thought held her still and controlled.

She had big shoes to fill after her predecessor, Jamieson, had retired, even though she knew she could fill the void he'd left behind. As a long-term member of the crew—over twenty years—his tenure on the *Star of Ishtar* had placed him aboard since its launch. Due to his experience in the heat of battle with the Ru'Edan he had made a name for himself as the coldest of cold in the hottest of situations. She hoped to emulate that herself and carve out her own place aboard the Ishtar, as its crew lovingly knew her.

Duvall and Grayson knew how much she wanted to prove herself. They just wouldn't have expected it here, on the Ishtar.

She watched Duvall study her, then, quickly turning on his heel, call to those assembled, "Dismissed."

Once they started to move away, she softened her stance, preparing to turn when the call came.

"Sudonne! A moment if you please."

Elara turned to face Duvall. "Commander?"

"Welcome to the *Star of Ishtar*, Elara. While I am surprised you're the new ST, Grayson and I are pleased you could join us. But how did you manage to pull it off? Keeping it quiet that you were the new ST?" he asked, his voice deep enough to make most women shiver with anticipation.

She smiled, thinking it was a shame she didn't have any feelings for him except sisterly attachment, but then again, given his lack of deep commitment to women, maybe it wasn't such a shame after all.

She understood what drove him. He wanted his own ship and to captain his own future. They'd spent many nights over wine or ale discussing his beliefs that commitment grounded a person. Inwardly, she shrugged. He'd make those calls for himself, though she was sure that one day he would come across someone who would make him consider his choices a little more thoroughly.

"I'm pleased to be here, Duvall. Having an uncle who happens to be an admiral, he was able to let Captain Elphin know that I wanted to surprise you. It's a small world in the Admiralty. Elphin already knew of me, so he okayed my placement. Once the powers knew there was no impediments to me joining the crew, it was fairly simple from there." She felt a small smile creep onto her face, then let it drop away. "What do you think Grayson thinks?"

"Ah, still chasing him, are you?" He grinned, his eyes twinkling. "I think he'll be pleased you're finally old enough and you're here." He looked her straight in the eye. "But you may just need to remind him of that particular fact." He motioned for her to go before him, barking out a deep laugh. "Come on, I'll show you to your cabin."

Available from Love Books Publishing
Available in Ebook via Books2Read

Direct Autographed Copy
https://www.imogenenix.net/Warriors1

The Blood Bride by Imogene Nix

Hope just wants to be an ordinary nestling. She went to college and escaped, but now she's back and there's a secret everyone is keeping from her.

Xavier is the new master of the nest, ready to welcome home the daughter of the house who he has never met. He's unprepared for the woman who steals his breath and enchants him.

Now Hope and Xavier must fight for lives and those of the innocents. After all, it is only by overcoming the rogues that they will have a chance of a timeless future together. But will it be in time?

PROLOGUE

As silence descended on the house, the shadows grew—dark grays and blacks that bled into each other. First one figure then another broke away, making a run toward the house. Silent as the grave, they moved swiftly over dew-slicked grass. Then they stopped still. Waiting. Not a movement betrayed them until a signal propelled them back into action and they started crawling upwards. The walls damp coating no barrier to the intruders that ascended in the darkness.

The sound of each window breaking shattered the quiet—the figures were inside. Screams echoed through the night. Yet, in this area of large estates, heavy with noise-absorbing shrubbery, no one could hear those within. The blood-curdling screams went on and on before finally dying away.

Just one sound echoed through the night: The sobbing of a child.

The front door opened and figures trooped out—ghostly specters against an inky night sky, broken by a single outline. A child in white, carried at the center of the pack.

No sound broke the silence as they moved toward the trees surrounded the house.

Flames now licked at the manor: A deathly glow of oily smoke rising.

All that remained was a single person—wrapped in a cape of midnight blue beyond the house—watching them melt away.

Jemima moved toward the burning structure, breaking into a run as she breached the threshold. Vainly she attempted to enter, but the heat drove her back.

Now dashing tears from her face, she raced across the graveled driveway toward the gates, where the guardhouse was located. No sign of life existed within the building and some instinct of survival slowed her pace to a careful creep. Out of breath and heaving from exertion, she nervously checked within.

Small puffs of white vapor colored the glass. She darted from one window to another. Her cloak drawn tightly around her body, hoping it would camouflage her from sight.

Satisfied, Jemima entered through the heavy, wooden front door and moved toward the phone she spied on the floor. Her eyes darting here and there she dialed, listening to the rotary motor as it returned to the proper position. Time was short and if *they* came back, she needed to have shared the message.

The phone rang once. Twice. With a brrping sound it connected.

"Hello?" A male answered and she felt a warm flush of relief at the voice. A voice she knew well.

"The manor has been breached. The girl child taken." The words erupted and her hand trembled.

"On our way." The click of the receiver being replaced echoed loudly in the stillness of the room.

Copper. She smelled copper.

Her stomach soured, knowing it meant more deaths. Jemima looked around for the gun—a gun with deadly, holy water-infused copper bullets—she knew was hidden somewhere in the room. A gun she couldn't find. *No divine intervention exists here*, she thought.

Hopefully *they* didn't remain. Feeding. If they were still here, that's what they would be doing. She found a corner and scrunched down, hiding from sight.

Crouched low, she tried to stay as still as possible, listening for sounds of the vehicles she knew would be coming. She dug her fingers into the flesh of her arms; remaining aware enough to stop before drawing blood. That would surely bring them out. Jemima dragged the cloak around her to capture the warmth, yet there was little to be found.

The sounds of engines roused her from the corner of the room. Jemima inched toward the window, the lead of the old glass distorting her view, hearing raised voices she knew Mistress Cressida had arrived.

Jemima retreated. Remained hidden from the woman because if she knew, all may well be lost. From the shadowed room she listened to the conversation...

"It smells like Estersham." The Mistress' eyes closed. "If it is, we have a problem." She turned once more, her face set and eyes now glacial in intensity. "James?"

The man nodded as if he knew what was to come.

"If I take those steps, I cannot return. Another must stand in my place." Her voice hardened while her eyes glittered in the dim light, piercing in their intensity.

Then the Mistress' voice called out in the near silence. "You and yours have been my loyal servants for so many years. I took an oath to protect you long ago. I renewed it with marriage and births, over and over. Now, my home and yours have been breached and this child taken from us. The girl child, who will be the hope and salvation of our kind, was ripped from the bosom of our nest. I will repay your loyalty and I will get her back." The words of power rippled in the night and licked at Jemima's skin.

Available in Ebook
books2read.com/BloodBride-Nix

Direct Autographed Copy
https://www.imogenenix.net/BloodBride

Also by Imogene Nix

<u>**Warriors of the Elector**</u>

- Star of Ishtar
- Starline
- Starfire
- Star of the Fleet
- Starburst
- The Star of Eternity

The Star of Ishtar & Starline - Print

Starfire & Star of the Fleet - Print

Starburst & The Star of Eternity - Print

The Secrets World:

Blood Secrets

- The Blood Bride
- The Illuminated Witch
- The Sorcerer's Touch

<u>**House Secrets**</u>

- As Dawn Breaks
- Immortal Consequences
- Unnamed Book III

All That Glitters - a House Secrets Novella (Coming in 2023)

<u>**Danu's Secrets**</u>

- The Downfall of Padraic O'Shaunessy (Coming in 2023)
- Unnamed Secrets Book II

The Automaton Series

- Haven House (Coming 2022)
- Nobel Crest (Coming 2022)

The Search Duology

- Miss Elspeth's Desire
- Miss Isabelle's Craving

Reunion Trilogy

- War's End
- The Assassin
- Executing Justice

The Reunion Trilogy in Paperback

Sex Love & Aliens

- Tangled Webs
- False Webs
- Covert Webs

21st Testing Protocol

- Cyborg: Redux
- Children Of A Greater Evil
- When Evil Came To Stay
- Finis: The War To End All Wars

Celtic Cupid Trilogy

- Blame The Wine
- A Stranger's Embrace
- Revenge On Cupid

The Celtic Cupid Trilogy in Paperback

Zombieology

- The Reset
- I Dream of Zombies
- The Six Million Dollar Zombie
- Make Room For Zombies (2022)
- Unnamed Zombiology Book (coming 2023)

Knights of Pleasure

- Silken Knights (Coming in 2022)

Single Titles

The Chocolate Affair (also in Print)

Falling In Love Again (Previously A Sapphire For Karina)

BioCybe (also in Print)

Hesparia's Tears (also in Print)

Tomorrow's Promise

A Bar In Paris (also in Print)

Inheritance Of The Blood (also in Print)

The Plan

Loving Memories (also in Print)

Hero of Heartbreak Hill (also in Print)

My One & Only

Curse Bound (coming 2021)

Raspberry Dreams (Not Yet Released)

Non Fiction

Self Publishing: Absolute Beginners Guide (With Suzi Love)

25 Curated Ways To Get Rid Of Telemarketers

Book Signings for Absolute Beginners

About the Author

Imogene is published in a range of romance genres including Paranormal, Science Fiction and Contemporary. She is mainly published in the UK and USA.

In 2010, Imogene Nix (the pen name not Imogene herself) was born. Imogene sat down and worked tirelessly for 3 months culminating in the book Starline, which became the first in a trilogy titled, "Warriors of the Elector." Since then she's had over 30 titles published and is now focusing on hybridising herself - with a mixture of traditionally published and self-published works.

In fact, she's taking control of many of her back catalogue books, which are slowly re-releasing as self-published titles.

Imogene is a member of a range of professional organisations world wide, and believes in the mantra of mentoring and paying it forward and is actively involved in mentorship (through NaNoWrimo and her vlog: In The Chair With Imogene Nix) and tutoring of new and upcoming authors.

In her spare time she loves to drink coffee, wine & eat chocolate and is parenting her spoiled dog and a ferocious cat along with her husband and 2 human daughters and looks forward to weekends away with her husband in their caravan "The Seven Year Hitch!" Do look forward to her caravan romance at some point!

To Contact Imogene
www.imogenenix.net
imogene@imogenenix.net

facebook.com/ImogeneNix

twitter.com/ImogeneNix

instagram.com/ImogeneNix

bookbub.com/authors/imogenenix